A woman moaned.

Blood spun around. The corridor was empty. He returned to the last door he'd passed. His pale fingers touched rough, pitted wood. The hinges were thick with rust, the bolt only slightly less so. Blood jiggled the bolt gently, pulling it free by centimeters. Rust flaked onto his hand, bright orange against colorless flesh. Blood made no more noise than a spider scuttling across a sheet of paper, and was displeased at being even that loud. His hand froze when the bolt slid free of its eye.

Slowly the vampire pulled the door open, ready to halt at the slightest creak. There was none. The hinges looked rusty, but their pivot pins had been recently oiled. He entered the cell.

The woman sat cross-legged on a soiled mattress against a side wall. Her hands were bound together at the wrists and held above her head by a length of bicycle chain looped through a steel eye imbedded in the wall. Her jeans were tattered shreds below the thigh. It was not easy to reconcile the haggard cheeks, dull eyes, and slack jaw with the beaming face of Arthur Blanchard's missing daughter, but chin and nose and ear shape did not lie. Sunlight streamed through a narrow barred window, striking Andrea Blanchard full in the face. Her head was, in fact, turned to receive its warmth on her tightly-drawn flesh. The glare prevented her from seeing her visitor clearly, but something—the slight breeze of the opening door, or the faint fetor of death that clung to the vampire—told her he was there.

She moaned again. Her dull eyes grew moist.

"Oh, god, already?" she sobbed.

THE SPY
WHO DRANK BLOOD

BY GORDON LINZNER

WASHINGTON D.C.

1984

ONE

Andrea Blanchard shivered as a breeze sliced the still, primeval Everglades night. She clenched her bruised jaw to keep her teeth from chattering, and the effort sent a flash of pain up the right side of her skull.

Her blouse hung open, buttons torn away, exposing goose-pimpling breasts to the damp air. She wished she could wrap her arms over them, for warmth, but her wrists were bound together, and tethered to a gnarled root of the mangrove tree against whose trunk she leaned. Every shift in position caused the heavy fishing rope to bite deeper into her skin. Her left hand was crudely bandaged with a blood-stained handkerchief. She settled deeper into the cold mud, which seeped through her cotton slacks.

Andrea glared at her five captors, drawing heat from the force of her hatred.

Within three paces of the woman, the quintet squatted in a tight circle, ignoring her, at ease in their isolation on this tiny, nameless island just outside Everglades National Park.

Four of the men wore full khaki uniforms, which bulged where gunbutts protruded from waistbands and extra cartridges jammed the pockets. The fifth man, Gary, who'd anglicized his first name from Garcia, stubbornly cherished denim jeans that fit too tight to provide decent insulation.

A match flamed in the center of the circle. Andrea turned away, feigning sleep, hoping to avoid their further attention. Her nose twitched. The harsh stench of burning tobacco joined the fetor of the surrounding swamp. She looked up cautiously. The tiny spot of red in the center of the circle vanished, reappeared, and vanished again, as the cigarette was passed from one shielding hand to the next.

One man waved it away without taking a pacifying drag. That was Sleet, tall, balding, and gaunt, who could cow each of his four subordinates with a glance from his copper-green eyes. Sleet had no time for smokes. He was absorbed in cleaning his rifle.

On Sleet's right, Gary grunted and passed the cigarette back the way it had come. From conversations overheard earlier, Andrea guessed that Sleet would not have so readily turned down a toke from a reefer, but marijuana was expressly forbidden during guard duty.

Gary grunted again, and shifted slightly to his right. "Watch your elbow, will you, Sleet? My whole left side is black and blue from being next to you."

"No one forced you to sit here." Sleet's voice was a hard-edged whisper, reminding Gary and the others that sound traveled far over water. "You could change places with Matt or Micky." Gary did not move, although the arches of his feet throbbed and his legs were going numb below the knees.

"Anyway," he continued, "isn't that gun clean enough? You've been playing with it for over an hour."

"The humidity here concerns me," Sleet explained, not pausing. "I'm not yet acquainted with this piece, and don't know how she'll react. A few drops of condensation inside the barrel could make her blow up in my face. I'll be surprised if your shotgun doesn't do just that, Matt." Sleet nodded to a chunky, red-haired man opposite him.

"Balls," spat Matt. "This baby has come through for me under tougher conditions."

"Don't know why you had to buy a new hunting rifle," added Micky, the former leader of a California motorcycle gang. "Seems an unnecessary risk, when we're getting a fresh shipment any day now."

Sleet's reply was a cold sting, befitting his name. "Snow approved the purchase. Do you question *his* judgment?"

"Of course not," Micky said hastily.

Andrea almost smiled, despite her swollen lip. She liked

to hear her captors bicker. She knew as well as any of them that Sleet had used every iota of his influence to obtain Snow's endorsement. He'd come within a hair's-breadth of overreaching himself and losing his position as second-in-command ... or possibly more. Sleet obviously felt the risk worthwhile. He was now the only member of the nightwatch with decent armament. Five handguns and a poorly-maintained shotgun did not inspire confidence.

"Generically," Sleet went on, "the only difference between this Remington and the Army version I used to have is in the fancy stock."

"And the registration number," added Matt.

"A problem I can deal with." Sleet laid the cleaning rod across his knees. He rubbed the back of his thigh to ease a forming cramp.

He'd hunkered down with the others two hours earlier, and had orders to remain so until dawn. The discipline of the squad was his responsibility. After the quarrel over the Remington, Sleet dared not take liberties with Snow's orders, however minor the breach. He shifted his weight from leg to leg to aid circulation, and continued squatting.

To Sleet's left sat curly-haired Tom, young enough to pass for a student. Tom was the one who'd first approached Andrea's camp on Holroyd Hummock. His infectious grin and sparkling eyes disarmed her. By the time Andrea realized the sparkle was not inspired by friendliness, his companions were closing in.

Tom's hand jerked up to slap the back of his neck. The sharp crack echoed over the marsh. A tree frog quit its love song and ducked into a muddy pond.

"Don't these fucking mosquitoes ever sleep?" Tom whined.

"They've finished their fucking," Micky said with a chuckle. "That's why they're so hungry." He took a thin cannister of insect repellent from his jacket pocket and dangled it between two fingers.

"Stuff doesn't work," Tom muttered, even as he accepted it. An aerosol hiss melded with the swamp sounds as he sprayed exposed flesh for the third time that night.

"Do your clothing, too," Sleet advised as he finished rubbing his leg. "It won't evaporate as quickly."

Matt shifted his shotgun to accept the cigarette coming his way again. "You sweat too much, Tom. It attracts them. You should relax more."

Sleet fixed Matt with a cold, green gaze the night could not dilute. The butt sizzled on hard-packed mud.

"He should be nervous," Sleet whispered. "All of us should. Even the others, back at the motel. I don't want to tell any of you again to keep your voices low. If you can't do that, then shut up. There shouldn't be anyone within miles of this spot, but that includes us. A Park Ranger, or even a poacher, could screw this operation properly."

"All right, Sleet," said Micky. "We're edgy. Waiting does that."

"Yeah," Matt added, "and since you mention getting screwed, maybe...."

Andrea ducked her head, feigning sleep. She knew at least one pair of eyes had turned to her. She could feel them jabbing at the yellow-black marks around her exposed breasts, moving down her torso to where the zipper of her slacks had jammed halfway.

She took no notice of Sleet's words. Each time her hopes of rescue were revived and dashed, they grew more pallid. It was easier to accept the situation than to endure continual disappointment.

The gag had been removed from her mouth long ago, leaving its bitter oily taste. Her throat was hoarse; she doubted she could work up a good yell. And what good would it do? No matter what Sleet said, Andrea strongly doubted anyone could hear her except her five captors.

"No," said Sleet. "She's had enough for tonight."

Amen to that, Andrea added silently.

A deep snort came from outside the circle.

Sleet brought up his Remington. His five round 7.62mm magazine snapped into place. He ignored the telescopic sight, which was useless under these conditions. Pity he hadn't persuaded Snow to spring for an infra-red Starlightscope as well.

At the same moment, Matt rammed two cartridges into his

shotgun. He spun around, low to the ground, under Sleet's line of fire.

The safeties of three handguns snicked off almost as one. Tom, Gary, and Micky took up positions as they'd been trained to do.

Then they waited.

Frogs croaked and peeped. A nesting limpkin cried indignantly. Ten eyes strained at the surrounding shadows.

Andrea drew a deep breath, and let it out in a slow wheeze. Twice earlier that night her captors had gone through this routine. Both times, the sounds had been of foraging animals. Andrea would believe in shining knights when she saw the white of their armor, and not before.

Water lapped the shore. Wind direction made it sound more distant than was possible. With the tide up, this island measured thirty-five meters at its widest.

"This time it's a 'gator!" said Tom. "I know it."

Sleet hissed at him. "You know shit. Probably some driftwood snagged by the tide. Besides, alligators don't attack grown men. Be still."

The lapping faded. In its place came a moist, sucking noise ending in a soft pop. Then the sucking again. Another pop.

Something moved through the muck at the edge of the hummock. Something coming toward their camp.

Sleet's palms slickened with perspiration. He eased his finger from the trigger and wiped his right hand on his thigh. Whatever it was that approached, it was not an alligator. And too heavy and noisy for a panther. Possibly a bear. Yes, that fit, though they should have come across the beast that afternoon when they'd scouted the hummock.

The rustling grew louder. It must be the largest bear the state of Florida had ever seen outside the circus wintering grounds.

Now the surrounding water dispersed the sounds. Sleet leaned forward and tapped Matt's shoulder. Matt looked back. Sleet pointed at two o'clock. Matt shook his head, his sights locked on a cypress tree dead ahead.

Sleet did not repeat his silent order. A good leader knows when not to press.

The swamp seemed to grow suddenly silent. Andrea tensed. *Something* was going on.

The roar of an automatic shattered the quiet. In the flash of light, the surrounding brush seemed to be rushing in. Then the swamp seemed darker than before. The others turned in the direction of the shot, unsure at first which of them had fired.

Gary screamed in terror. "Madre Dias!"

"There!" Sleet rasped.

Andrea saw it first. She flattened as much as her tether allowed, hoping it was enough to save her from the impending crossfire. Gary hung silhouetted against the night sky, two meters above soggy ground. He kicked out wildly, dangling by khaki lapels.

A huge, muddy, shambling thing held him aloft.

The creature stood half again a man's height, and as thick as an ancient mangrove. In the darkness, caked mud seemed to roll down its swollen limbs.

Gary yelped as he was hoisted higher. His arms flailed. He hung limp above the thing's head.

Tom was closest. He couldn't miss. He steadied his shooting hand with the other and pumped bullet after bullet into the thing's gut. The weapon clicked four times before Tom realized it was empty.

The huge form neither fell nor staggered. Tom might as well have pelted it with feathers. But he had accomplished something.

He'd made it mad.

Roaring, the creature turned to him. Its warm, sour breath churned Tom's stomach. Fear locked the young man's muscles; he could not even fumble for fresh ammunition. Only when Gary's body came hurtling at him did Tom find the strength to react.

He was too slow.

Gary's boot-heel caught Tom in the temple. He fell flat, dazed. The gun flew from his fingers. He did not move.

"You walking shitpile!" snarled Matt. He discharged one barrel of the shotgun into the thing's side. The second shot went wild. Matt was yanked from the ground as easily as Gary had been.

Matt swung his shotgun like a club. The creature ducked its head; the stock cracked against its shoulder. Matt dropped the useless weapon and tugged desperately at his jacket buttons, cursing the quality of the Army surplus material. Why didn't the lousy cloth tear?

Sleet took care to aim his Remington 700. He hated wasting ammunition. His bullet sank into the thing's shoulder.

Success! This time the roar was tinged with pain!

Sleet wasted no time celebrating. He shifted the bolt. The next bullet slid into place. In a fraction of a second, it followed the first.

In that same fraction of a second, the creature swung Matt around.

The second bullet tore through Matt's back. Matt gurgled, stiffening. His bowels loosened.

Sleet instinctively peered through the sight for a clear and, he hoped, final shot. A head shot should do it. His field of vision was constricted. He could not see Matt's corpse flying toward him.

The impact swung Sleet around. He grunted, and landed face down in a shallow, muddy pool. Matt lay across his shoulders, pinning him down, leaking dark, glistening fluid.

Micky emptied a .38 revolver. Some of the bullets struck the creature. Some did not. It did not make much difference.

Now Micky wished he'd chosen an automatic from their small arsenal. He'd gladly exchange his weapon's advantages in fire power for a fast-loading cartridge. His dirt-stained fingers jammed into a side pocket, tearing open a box of bullets. He touched the cool, smooth, steel jackets, but knew there wasn't enough time to reload. The creature was too close.

The gun was useless, anyway. Throw it at the thing, and hope it provides enough distraction to let him get away.

Micky raised his hand.

A huge gnarled hand enclosed both Micky's fingers and the weapon. Micky screamed. He screamed again as the hand squeezed shut. Bones cracked. Flesh was mangled against metal. Micky tried to scream again, and managed a barely audible squeak. The pain had sapped all his energy. He fainted, held

horribly erect by the inhuman grip on his mutilated hand.
Andrea lay still, hardly daring to breathe. Her body made
tiny, jerking movements, as if trying to burrow into the mud for
concealment. Her wrists bled as the fishing rope dug into them.
A flying wood chip had scratched her hand, but as far as she
could tell no bullet had come close to her.

The creature stood absolutely still, as though posing with a
trophy in its outstretched hand. Its blazing yellow eyes scanned
the campsite. The lipless mouth curled as if to smile, revealing
rows of uneven, razor-sharp teeth. A deep grunt escaped its
throat.

Dragging Micky as if he were a pull-toy, the creature lumbered over to two of its four victims. With its free hand, it
dragged Matt's bleeding carcass off Sleet. The green-eyed leader
of the group had been the only one of the five to hurt the creature, even slightly, and that qualified him for special attention.

The creature flipped Sleet over and glared at his face. After
a moment, the man was dropped back into the pool with a
splash. The yellow eyes glimmered with displeasure. The col-
lision with Matt had driven the air from Sleet's lungs and the
next breath automatically sucked in muddy water. The man had
drowned in a few millimeters of puddle.

The thing turned toward his two other victims, then paused.
A flash of white caught its eyes: Andrea's hands, held aloft by
her short tether.

Still dragging Micky, the creature approached. Andrea
shuddered at the first slimy touch on her arm. The thing fingered the tether, and Andrea saw that it really had a hand and
not some modified paw. The appendage was swollen and misshapen, but definitely anthropic.

It twisted the rope and snapped it one-handed, as easily as
Andrea could have broken a thread. Unable to stand, much less
run from this apparition, the woman let it lift her over its right
shoulder. The cool, slippery skin of the creature caused her
hair to prickle, but on reflection it was no worse than the mud
she'd been sitting in, which now caked her back. And a definite
improvement over the clammy, greasy, probing touch of Sleet
and his associates.

The creature shifted its bulk. Andrea feared she would be dropped, but one massive hand wrapped tight about her calves, holding her in place. The creature was hauling Micky onto the other shoulder. The weight of the stocky former motorcycle gangleader counterbalanced her own.

Micky's shattered hand flopped near her face. Andrea shut her eyes and turned away, swallowing as hard as her bruised throat allowed. She didn't want to vomit; not in this awkward position.

"What next?" she muttered, doubting she would survive the night.

The answer came in a slurred, low-pitched voice: "Patience. I've plans for you both."

She quickly turned to Micky. He was still in a deep faint. But if Micky hadn't spoken, then …

Then the creature had.

Andrea let her mind sink into black insensibility.

TWO

On September 4, 1958, Congressman Erich Nash died in his sleep.

Three years later, a special agent with the code name of Blood was killed while on assignment in the Balkans.

Less than a year after that, Blood moved into the late Congressman's home.

The two story frame house sits in the middle of a quiet residential block in Washington, D.C., outwardly very much like its neighbors. Inside, as stipulated by the Congressman's will, the original files and documents accumulated by Nash in more than twenty years of political life are preserved. Few visitors consult them. The yellowing papers are available at any time on microfilm at the Library of Congress, while Arthur Blanchard, appointed custodian of these archives, is very difficult to reach. Researchers are welcomed by appointment only.

Yet Arthur Blanchard is very well paid, for a custodian.

In March of 1962, neighbors on either side of the Nash house won paid vacations in Hawaii, through a national magazine sweepstakes. Workmen moved swiftly. When the families returned a month later, the Congressman's self-dedicated monument looked exactly the same. The additions were made wholly underground. The hand-picked construction crew was disbanded immediately, and warned never to meet each other again. Three separate architecture firms had drawn up the plans, each unaware of the others' parts, and of the nature and actual location of the substructure.

A narrow passageway leads from Nash's basement and beneath the street to a two-room complex. The smaller room, at the far end, holds several electrical and refrigeration elements, but most of its space is taken up by a box of reinforced glass. In size and shape and one more important feature, it resembles a transparent coffin.

The box was constructed to the specifications of Professor Carl Russell, when he was head of government research into cryology. Russell believed that a major breakthrough in technique would allow him to freeze and revive a fully grown human being within a matter of years. The medical implications were enormous.

The Pentagon saw some intriguing possibilities, as well, and pressed for early results.

They pressed too hard. Federal prisoners were offered to Russell for experimentation. He refused. He used himself as a guinea pig.

In the nearly two decades since Russell's death, despite great advances, individual body organs still could not be frozen and thawed without cell damage. Even less could a living collection of such organs survive intact. Different cell types require different temperatures, cooling rates, and freezing methods. If only one cell is damaged by improper freezing or thawing, the spoilage quickly spreads.

As a result, one anonymous cryologist stated that with present methods and technology a frozen body stood less chance of being successfully revived in the future than an embalmed corpse.

That grisly irony appealed to the man who lay naked within the glass case. His form was indistinct, concealed by the liquid nitrogen that halted his chemical and biological processes, and by the thin frost layer lining the coffin. The chamber was chilly, but still much warmer than the box interior.

Since 1962, the man had been frozen and revived many times, with routine success. Unfortunately, this achievement did not vindicate Professor Russell.

The man in the case was dead.

With him died his real name. When active, he used a variety of code names, but he only thought of one of those names as truly his.

The name was Blood.

Blood woke.

Frost slowly retreated from the glass lid of the coffin. Fresh air, sharp and cold, was pumped into the case. The liquid nitrogen that kept Blood's body at a constant -196° Celsius was drained off. Hearing was the first sense Blood was aware of as he came to, but the soft whisper of machinery was barely audible, even to him. Not until his eyelashes thawed enough to separate, and he stared past ice-streaked glass at the featureless white ceiling, was Blood certain he was being revived.

His thin lips twitched. It felt good to be needed again.

He flexed the stiffness from the joints of his long, pale fingers. He moved his arms up and back, bending slowly at the elbow, raising his hands to press flat palms against the lid. He pushed. The glass resisted. His thawing muscles increased the pressure.

Crack! The last of the frost gave way. The cover slid easily along its grooved edges until Blood lay exposed from head to crotch.

The hands moved to the slick sides of the case. Blood pulled himself to a sitting position. His hairless chest quivered as he sucked warm outer air into thawing lungs. Blood did not need oxygen to survive, but he had to have air passing through his throat in order to speak. In addition, not breathing seemed to have a disconcerting effect on the living, who were aware of something missing but couldn't quite decide what.

How long had it been this time? A month? A year? Five years? Blanchard had originally hung a calendar in the room, but Blood had torn it down. He wanted no distractions at this point.

His one concern on waking was to satisfy the hunger that gnawed at his vitals; the need that coursed through his collapsed, depleted veins. The slow freezing that induced his biologically inert state also dehydrated his body cells, and a heavy concentration of salt formed in their interiors. This left him parched. A quick freezing would have solved that, but it would also have formed ice crystals, destroying delicate membranes. Blood healed with preternatural speed, without a scar, from wounds that would have been fatal to a living man, but as far as he knew he could not replace any organ that a normal person couldn't.

It did not matter whether Blood was frozen for an hour or a decade. The desire for fresh blood superseded all else in those first few minutes.

He clambered from the glass case and lunged for the shelf on the wall. Here sat half a dozen glass cannisters of thick, dark red liquid. Hands like claws grasped the nearest. Blood tore at the rubber lid. It snapped off, springing through the air to land somewhere behind him. Scarlet fluid spilled down his throat. Neck muscles pulsed. A trickle escaped to dribble on his chin and drip onto his bare, white chest.

The shatterproof canister thudded on the floor, and already Blood was scrabbling at a second. The third was nearly empty when his movements at last became less frantic.

Chilled blood was a poor substitute for the rich warm nectar that flowed from living veins, but it took the edge off Blood's physical craving. He likened the effect to that of methadone, which eases the agony of heroin deprivation without the incapacitating high. Blood grew rational now, almost in full control of his vampiric instincts. He calmly peeled the lid from one more cannister, and sipped slowly.

Four cannisters! He shook his head as he placed the last empty on the shelf. The bloodlust was becoming worse, perhaps aggravated by the cryogenic process. One day it might be completely out of control.

Arthur Blanchard kept an ash-wood stake against that day.

Blood tapped his index finger on the lid of a fifth canister. The rubber made a hollow sound that echoed in the room. Exerting his will, the agent jerked his hand away. He turned to stare at the chamber's single, narrow door.

It was made of twenty-centimeter-thick steel, and depended on a sequence of balance mechanisms for its time-locked release. Blood's inhuman strength could eventually tear through it, but that would take longer than the few minutes until the door opened of its own accord. Such an act would only alert Blanchard or whoever was monitoring his revival that he'd finally gone berserk. There were contingency plans in that event. Blood did not wish to learn what they were.

The multiple clicks of the lock disengaging sounded like a ball bearing bouncing down a flight of stairs. When the bearing hit bottom, the door slid open silently.

In the center of the antechamber was a coffee table, on which Blood's briefing materials were usually placed. There was also a washstand and towel to permit the agent to remove the evidence of his hasty thirst-quenching; since mirrors were useless, he had to guess at his appearance. Finally, there was the straight-backed chair with its neat pile of fresh clothing, and a beige cotton sports jacket hung over the back. Another warm weather assignment, he surmised.

This room's ambient temperature was twenty degrees Celsius, to help speed Blood's thawing. The agent was indifferent. Frigid air followed him into the room, condensing into wispy clouds. The door of the cryogenic chamber slid shut behind him. He took his time padding in bare feet across the metal floor.

The time-lock on the outer door was set for an additional ten minutes.

He scowled as he reached the table. There were no files, no reports, no photographs or documents or instructions to memorize and destroy. Instead, there was a single sheet torn from a desk calendar, dated December 5, 1979. Only a few months, then, since the Philippines job.

He turned it over. The message was penciled in block letters:

My office.
A.B.

Blood's lips drew back in a snarl, revealing the canine fangs. Blanchard knew better than this. Blood wanted his assignments impersonally; he'd insisted on it when they'd first established procedure. The living felt uncomfortable in his presence, especially those few who knew his secret. Even Arthur Blanchard. For his own part, Blood was never wholly at ease with their kind. More than his fellow agents, he had to continually pretend to be what he was not; what he had been but could never be again.

Blood had severed every connection with his prior existence, even renouncing his name; every connection save one. As official custodian of the Nash archives and, of course, secret head of the security organization called the Office, Arthur Blanchard had been Blood's superior since the mid-1950's. Blanchard was the only man Blood could turn to, when he realized what fate had made of him. It was only natural that Blanchard be given charge when special cases came up that called for Blood's unique talents.

But there had never been a need to discuss the assignment face to face.

Blood crumpled the calendar page into a tight ball, and kept his powerful fingers clenched tightly about it. There had better be a good reason for this sudden change.

He dropped the ball gently on the table. Unless Arthur Blanchard had lost his touch in the past seventeen years, there'd be a damned good reason.

THREE

Through slitted eyelids, Tom watched the creature shoulder its victims and vanish into the thick undergrowth.

A thousand insects fed on Tom's face and hands and the exposed section of calf where the pants leg had slid from the boot top. Cold, muddy water seeped into the boots and through thick cotton socks; it felt like ice against his toes and ankles. Eyes watered. Forehead throbbed. Needles shot through his left leg, which was pinned to the sodden ground.

Tom continued to lay there long after the splashes faded. He dared not move so much as a pinky. Even his breathing was shallow. The sounds of departure could have been a trick. The thing might still lurk just out of sight behind a mangrove, or be hunched over in a patch of sawgrass, watching for a sign of life it had not already snuffed out.

Certainly Snow would not have left the job unfinished … why should this creature be different?

At last, Tom worked up the courage to open his eyes fully. He took in the surroundings with care; no sudden pupil shifts to attract attention. There was a soiled boot on the right of his face. Its toe pointed at the overhanging branches. The heel was half-buried in ooze.

So far, so good. He shifted his head. The throbbing flared, then faded. His neck felt stiff, but at least it wasn't broken. He wriggled his fingers. They buried themselves in the soft earth like fat white grubs. He clenched his fist. Mud squirted from between his fingers. The sensation was strangely comforting.

When these tiny movements drew no attention, Tom grew bolder. He rolled onto his stomach, freeing his leg from the pressing weight. He winced at the myriad aches this awoke.

The boot by his face contained a foot, which led to a leg, a torso, and finally a blood-streaked face. Gary. From the way the body was twisted, Tom knew Gary's spine was broken. It was Gary's other leg, nothing more, that had weighted down Tom's limb.

Tom pushed up shakily onto hands and knees. He tasted the sour burning in the back of his throat, and swallowed back the vomit. He crawled three paces to a cypress tree and used its trunk to haul himself erect. His fingernails gouged the bark as he stood there, waiting for the swamp to stop spinning.

He wondered if the concussion would prove fatal. Then he wondered whether it mattered.

The relief guard would be arriving in a few hours, at dawn, and Tom had a mental image of himself explaining what had happened ... first to the guard, and then to Snow himself. He'd seen how Snow dealt with liars and traitors ... or those Snow thought were liars and traitors. The truth was too fantastic, even with the broken bodies for verification.

He couldn't stay here, waiting for the relief ... or for the monster to return.

Of course, Snow would search for him, as he would search for Micky and their stolen captive. But he couldn't be sure that there wasn't some perfectly ordinary explanation for their disappearance; that, for instance, a carrion-starved alligator hadn't dragged their bodies to its den. And Snow could ill afford to stay in one spot for more than a few weeks at most. Surely Tom could hide for that long in a hundred thousand hectares of swamp. Escaped slaves and convicts had been doing so for hundreds of years.

All Tom had to do was avoid the twenty plus men in Snow's command ... and that thing.

But first he had to stop his legs from wobbling.

FOUR

"The snow just started falling," said Arthur Blanchard. He stood by a window, his fingers holding the edge of a drawn, heavy curtain, making just enough of a gap for one eye to peer through. Flakes whirled in the glow of a streetlamp on the deserted sidewalk. "Please be seated, Blood."

The agent crossed the thick pile carpet noiselessly. The wood paneling and thick draperies made the room seem darker than it was. The only interior light came from the high-powered lamp on Blanchard's desk.

"Will it stick?" asked Blood.

"No. This is only a flurry."

Blood settled into a chair of dark brown leather, facing the scarred oak desk. "This is luxurious, after all that glass and metal. Can you have padding installed in my coffin?"

Blanchard let the curtain fall shut. He turned to his visitor. The desk lamp etched deep shadows in Blood's pale features.

"At that temperature it would freeze hard as metal. You'd be no better off."

"But it's the thought that counts."

Blanchard shuffled to his desk, iron-gray eyes downcast. He sensed Blood following his smallest move. He gripped the arms of his chair too firmly as he lowered into it. When he clasped his hands atop the desk, the thumbs drummed unbidden. Blanchard had rehearsed a dozen openings to this exchange. He now rejected all of them.

Blood stared calmly at him. The silence grew tangible.

"I'm not sure how to start this, Jim."

"Start by calling me Blood," the agent snarled.

The thumbs froze in mid-beat. Blood's sudden ferocity startled the man. Hairs rose on the back of his neck. "I'm sorry. I'm not used to this. It's been a long time since we've talked."

"You should be glad I'm so unsociable," Blood replied, forcing a lighter tone. "Otherwise I might throw in with bad company. Axe-murderers, baby-rapists, politicians."

A corner of Blanchard's mouth twitched, acknowledging the jest. "A grateful nation applauds you."

The hard edge returned to Blood's voice. "Then why the sudden urge for a chat, after all these years?"

Blanchard unclasped his hands and rubbed a thumbnail along his upper lip. It was a habit he'd never quite broken, although habits could be fatal in his work. Blanchard hadn't sported a mustache since Malenkov was the Russian Premier. That was the year his wife announced her loathing of facial hair.

"You once met my daughter, Andrea." There was a gilt-framed photograph on the corner of the desk. Blanchard turned it towards Blood.

The vampire's lips became a thin, almost invisible line. He detested reminders of his breathing days … as Arthur Blanchard well knew. "Operation Smoke," he replied. "Six round-the-clock agents to protect your family. The little girl was my personal responsibility. It lasted a month. The threats were idle."

"At the time, we had to take them seriously. The Senate was investigating the John Birch Society. Several attempts had been made to steal some of Senator Nash's records, which were being used in evidence."

Blanchard paused. He was starting to relax now. If he could have kept the conversation on the level of shop talk, there'd be no sense of anxiety. But if he could have done that, he wouldn't have needed to speak to Blood at all.

The vampire picked up the photograph, studied it, replaced it and turned it to face Blanchard again. He said nothing. His face was expressionless.

"As you see," Blanchard continued, "Andrea's a big girl now. She took a bachelor's degree in journalism last year. I offered to help find her a job. She landed one without me."

"Washington Post? New York Times?"

Blanchard sighed and shook his head. "Andrea was too impatient to work her way up on a prestige newspaper. Have you heard of the Weekly Examiner?"

"No."

"It started up about six years ago; one of those sensationalist tabloids you see at supermarket checkout counters."

Blood lifted an eyebrow. "I don't shop very often."

"The Examiner *has* run a few valid exposes. Law of averages. Andrea saw a chance for a byline on a big scandal that would turn her into the next Carl Bernstein. Instead, she's out interviewing astrologers, psychic healers, flying saucer contactees...."

Blood permitted himself a faint smile. "Have you introduced her to Allen Davies?"

Blanchard winced at the name. Davies was a young man with an influential uncle and a hunger for the glamour of espionage ... as well as a complete lack of common sense. In consequence, he was bounced from one security organization to another. When it was the Office's turn, Blanchard assigned Davies to a simple courier task ... and then Blood had to retrieve the microfilm from a trench at the bottom of the South China Sea.

"What's happened to your daughter?" Blood continued.

Blanchard drew a deep breath. "Two weeks ago she went down to the Florida Everglades, which anyone could have discovered by calling the paper. There's been a rash of skunk-ape sightings.

"They call it a skunk-ape down there, and usually the reports come from the Florida panhandle. Similar creatures have been reported throughout the world under a host of names: the Fouke monster, Sasquatch, Yeti, the Jersey Devil, Bigfoot."

"The Jersey Devil was confessed as a hoax eighty years ago."

Blanchard shrugged. "Tell the man who thinks he's seen one. That's just the background. I don't give a damn if the Fontainebleau is hosting a Missing Link convention. I want you to look at this." Blanchard slowly took a small, white pill box from a desk drawer, and slid it across the polished oak to within Blood's reach. His voice had begun to break at the last sentence, and his lower lip quivered.

Blood reached out and lifted the lid. Inside the box, a pale, gray, worm-like thing rested on a wad of cotton. He plucked it out. Blanchard turned to stare at the curtain. After a moment of scrutiny the agent replaced the thing and closed the box. He slid it back to Blanchard gently.

"Her editor in Chicago called the house," Blanchard said. "Andrea had failed to send in her story on time. A day later, this box came by special delivery. They called within an hour of its arrival."

The vampire adopted his most detached tone. "I saw traces of ink on the tip. You compared it with her records?"

"Of course. It's Andrea's. There's agreement in thirty different points, more than enough for a court of law." He placed the box back in its drawer, which he slowly shut. "The left pinky."

Blood pursed his lips. "What do they want?"

"The release of three terrorists from an Ohio penitentiary."

Blood rose, towering over the older man. "Why you? Only a handful of people, above and below you, know your real function."

Blanchard cleared his throat. "A terrorist group calling themselves the Free Thought Alliance have over the past two years claimed responsibility for dozens of bombings and several sniping incidents throughout the northeast. The Cleveland police department received information this summer about a weapon cache in that city, and notified Washington. On behalf of the Office, I was ordered to help co-ordinate the raid."

Blood sank back into his chair and stared into Blanchard's iron gray eyes. "You went in person?"

"Damn it, Blood!" Blanchard slammed a fist down heavily on the scarred desk top. "The White House put the screws on. A Pakistani diplomat was killed in one of the Alliance's New York explosions. Top men from every security outfit were ordered to be on hand!"

Blood resisted an urge to smile as Blanchard's pallid cheeks flashed crimson. The man had fire in him yet. "Could Davies's uncle have arranged for your involvement, getting even for canning his nephew?"

"I have no evidence." Blanchard turned away. He wondered

how the flurry outside was doing, but did not get up to look. "We discovered a veritable bomb factory in Cleveland, along with seven FTA members. Three were killed in a gun-battle. One of the remaining four, Rodicio Chavez, tried to blow up the building with ourselves inside, but he miscalculated. Chavez lost both hands and half his face, including an eye; none of our people were even scratched by the blast. Aside from our own forces, only those four survivors knew I'd directed the raid. They've been held incommunicado since then."

"Somebody talked to someone," Blood stated.

Blanchard licked his lips. "Last month, Chavez escaped. He'd been transferred to a state hospital to be fitted with prosthetic hands. He didn't wait; his first night there, he eluded his guards and climbed out a second story window." Blanchard met Blood's incredulous stare. "Informants tell me the Cleveland police let him escape, hoping he would lead them to the rest of the Alliance. A cripple like Chavez would be easy to shadow."

"Apparently not easy enough."

Blanchard nodded. His features seemed to sag.

"You mentioned a phone call," Blood prompted.

"A local call, too brief to trace. Probably relayed by someone in Washington. I assume they're holding her in the Everglades area."

"And you agreed to their demands at once."

"Naturally. And I have three separate contingency plans for the release of those men and ultimately the capture of the kidnappers. I needed only the second phone call, in which arrangements would be made, to set my plans in motion." Blanchard stared at his desktop.

"The call never came," Blood surmised.

Blanchard sighed. "The call never came. And the people above me *refuse* to let me take further action until it does. They say it's a hoax, or an Examiner publicity gag, or a glory play on my part. At my age! With my record! As if that finger could be faked!"

Blood rose smoothly and stepped around the desk. He placed a hand on the older man's shoulder. The vampire's touch was, of course, cold as ice, but Blanchard's jacket absorbed most of the chill. The weight of the hand calmed him.

"I'm all right," Blanchard said at last. "Please, sit down. There's more."

"I thought there would be," Blood replied, backing away.

"I couldn't just sit on my thumbs, with Andrea's life at stake. I asked my Miami representative, Frank Jordan, to sniff around unofficially. Three days ago he said he had a line on Andrea's sources. I sent back word to forget the story and look for the kidnappers. He never received it. No one's seen him since." Blanchard leaned forward, elbows on desk.

"I'm to find Andrea and rescue her."

If she still lived. They both knew how remote that possibility was. Something had gone sour on the Alliance's end, and that's why they hadn't called. Perhaps she'd died unexpectedly. Perhaps someone had gotten suspicious, and they'd had to get rid of the woman fast. Blood might be too late to save Blanchard's daughter, but he'd know how to deal with her slayers.

He'd just follow his vampiric instincts.

Blanchard stared down at the desktop. The knuckles of his clenching fists whitened. "I can't order you to do this. Officially, I can't even ask you. It would have to be a personal favor." He licked his lips. "Every time you leave this house, Blood, there's a chance your true nature will be exposed. I don't have to tell you what the first step in a cover-up would be if that news leaked out … especially on an unsanctioned mission. If you want to return to your ice box in the basement now, I won't hold it against you."

"The hell you won't." Blood eased his body back in the leather chair. He stretched his long arms and widened his mouth in a mock yawn, baring his canine fangs. "It's too soon to go back to sleep. Besides, you knew I'd agree before you defrosted me."

"I'd hoped. I had to ask." From another desk drawer Blanchard removed a thick wallet-sized folder. "Reservations have been made on flight 726. It's due to stopover in Dulles on its way to Miami within the hour, if the weather doesn't delay it. Everything I've told you, and quite a bit I haven't, is in those papers. You're a reporter for the occult magazine *Heaven and Earth* … unless you've a better idea?"

Blood leafed through the folder, shaking his head. "I won't

have any ideas until I've started. If Jordan got a line by tracing Andrea's trail, I can, too. Otherwise I'll try following *his* tracks. You've no idea of what he'd found, or thought he'd found?"

"None at all. We had a team search his apartment, the usual procedure, but they came up empty."

"Let's hope a native picked up something he doesn't know what to do with. My name is Al Cuardi?"

Blanchard offered an apologetic shrug. "Fred Newman's still handling your code names. Sometimes I think he's in the wrong business. Spell that backwards, invert two letters, and...."

"I saw it. I like Fred's sense of humor, but one day he'll get too obvious for comfort."

"You should see the names I screen out."

"I'd like to, some day." Blood slipped the folder into his jacket pocket, stood up, and walked to the door of Blanchard's office. No handshake, no luck-wishing; he'd had enough human contact for the moment.

The agent paused at the open door and looked back at Blanchard. The older man sat erect behind the desk, hands once more tightly clasped, face washed out in the harsh glow of the desk lamp.

"There's no chance Andrea will recognize me, is there?"

Blanchard sighed. "I doubt it. She was only a toddler. I don't recall her ever mentioning you after Operation Smoke was terminated."

"I thought not." Blood toyed with the doorknob, rattling it in his long, pale fingers. "That's all right, then. Fine."

Then he was gone.

FIVE

An Everglades night could seem eternal, but Lucille Hernandez knew better. She paused beside an ancient mangrove tree and rolled back the dark green sleeve of her park ranger uniform. The luminous dial of her wristwatch was exposed for less than a second. Ten minutes past four. Not long until first light.

For over an hour she'd followed an artless trail through the cool, dank swamp. Now she heard the blazer of that trail ahead of her. Obviously an amateur. She'd have caught the poacher already if she hadn't taken time to haul the maimed doe to a compound and patch her up.

Hernandez unholstered the automatic at her hip and closed in. Her silent approach through the thick brush was in marked contrast to her prey's thrashing. Some of her stealth was inherited from her Seminole mother, but most of it came from long hours of self-training intended to make her the best park ranger in the state.

Hernandez was glad that she, and not her assistant, Bill Arneson, had been on late patrol tonight. Not that she'd have begrudged him the capture. Bill was bright and willing to put in long hours, but a forestry degree was no substitute for woodcraft experience. And Bill always stayed within the boundaries of Everglades National Park. Hernandez preferred stalking the perimeter, sometimes in the park and sometimes in territory under the official jurisdiction of Sheriff Paul Rudge.

The doe was found at the edge of the park, which was good enough for Hernandez. The arrow that had torn its tendons could have been fired on park grounds, or the animal might have been driven from its sanctuary. Hernandez issued weekly memos requesting more funds for fence repair. If anyone read them, the news hadn't filtered back to her.

Sheriff Rudge was easy to get along with, once he was convinced she knew her job. He didn't mind her encroaching on his bailiwick, and she wouldn't raise a stink if he had to invade park land. She'd even invite his help on a tough problem.

A single off-season poacher, firing arrows so crude they could only cripple a doe, was not a tough problem.

A twig snapped three meters ahead of her. A shape moved against the dark, intertwined vegetation. Quietly, Hernandez released her automatic's safety. She was invisible for the moment, but that was going to change quickly.

She let the poacher gain a couple of meters, preferring to confront him—for some reason, poachers were always male—outside the dense foliage. It was too easy for a man to slip away with this much cover. The ranger wanted a wide clearing, where he could not duck a bullet. There was such a space less than a kilometer forward, if her mental map was accurate.

It was. Ten minutes later, Hernandez peered around the thick and twisted trunk of a cypress. A slim form stepped from the brush. His khaki pants were tattered below the knees, and his flannel shirt hung in ribbons. A hand-made bow was held at the ready, but even in the dim moonlight the ranger saw no arrow poised. He turned his head, showing Hernandez a ragged profile. Clumps of matted hair topped a dirt-smeared, pasty face.

"Shit," Hernandez muttered. "He's just a kid."

She entered the clearing.

The kid spun around, for Hernandez abandoned her stealth. His free hand snatched at one of the three arrows tucked in his waistband. Then he saw moonlight glint on Hernandez's gun barrel, and changed his mind.

"Parks Department. Freeze or I'll shoot."

His knees bent as he prepared to run. Hernandez fired over his head, and made a flourish of aiming lower. The second shot would end his running days.

"All right, lady. I'm fucking froze, already!" He dropped the bow and raised his hands over his head.

Keeping the gun and one eye on her prisoner, the ranger moved forward to recover the bow. She slid it over her left shoulder, scowling disapproval at the excess slack of the string. The kid must've been almost on top of the doe to achieve what penetration he had with this weapon. A halfway decent hunter would have slain the animal instantly.

"You probably *are* frozen, in those rags," she said.

"I can take it."

"A Spartan. Good. What's your name?"

"I don't have to tell you."

"And I don't have to blow off your kneecaps, but I will if you don't tell me."

He sniffed. "Tom."

"That's saved one knee."

"Ah, Mason. Tom Mason."

The ranger's lips formed a tight smile. "You lie lousy, kid, but it beats John Doe. You can get away with it for now. I want you to pull those arrows out of your belt, Tom. One at a time, using only two fingers. Make a nice pile there in front of you."

Tom obeyed, glumly. The arrows were no great loss; he was no better at fashioning them than at making a bow.

"I was hungry. I'm still hungry." The Everglades was a riot of flora and fauna, but Tom had no idea what plants were safe to eat, and which would kill him in minutes. The Houston public school system had never taught him that.

"You're in luck, kid. Not only do you get to spend the rest of tonight in a nice warm holding cell, but there's free breakfast on the county. In fact, you'll probably draw three squares for at least the next thirty days. Unless you can pay the fine?"

Tom shook his head.

"I thought not. Don't give me a hard time, and I'll try to give you a break. Now step back. I want to collect the rest of my evidence."

Tom stepped back one pace; then, unbidden, another. Hernandez scowled and waved her gun.

"Please," he said. The surly tone was gone. Something other than Hernandez's .45 was scaring him. "Take the bow and

arrows. I won't hunt any more. But don't take me in. They'll
find out where I am. They'll think I betrayed them."

The ranger let the arrows be. "They?"

Tom shuddered.

"Who are they, Tom? Your parents?"

"You don't know what they're like, what they can do."

Wonderful, Hernandez thought. She should have guessed
the kid was a mental case. Wandering dangerous swamplands
at night, dressed in rags, trying to down game with a home-
made weapon that was barely more effective than a rubber-
tipped dart. Paranoid delusions were icing on the cake. The situation called for great tact, a quality Hernandez did not possess
in abundance.

"It's all right. They won't find you, not where we're going."

Cautiously, Hernandez stretched out her left hand. Tom
shrank from it. "They can go anywhere. Snow can do anything."

Hernandez took a deep breath. "This is southern Florida,
kid. We don't get snow. Come on. It's a long walk back."

Tom's head jerked to the side. "Hear that?"

The ranger groaned. "That won't work on me, Tom."

"Will you fucking shut up? You're going to get me killed.
You'll get us both killed. He'll hear us."

"Plenty of quiet in a holding cell, Tom. Come along. No one
is going to get you." She gestured impatiently.

Tom ran his tongue over dry lips.

The ranger's eyes narrowed. "How long have you been out
here, Tom?"

"God knows. Hours like days. Days like weeks."

"Yeah. You've picked up some kind of bug. You're feverish.
I'm going to get you to a doctor quick."

Tom still did not move.

Hernandez puffed out her cheeks in exasperation. She
couldn't stand here all night chatting with a madman. Nor
could she shoot him in cold blood, just to provoke a reaction
…although the idea was tempting. Maybe he'd trust her more
if she lowered the gun. Her reflexes had to be better than his.
Holding the weapon to one side, she stepped forward and
touched his elbow.

Tom yelped like a scalded puppy and bolted across the clearing.

"Freeze, goddamn it!" Hernandez fired over his head. This time Tom wasn't stopping. She aimed lower. She had a clear shot. She had time for several clear shots, following the youth with her gun until he vanished into a stand of trees. But she did not fire them.

"Crap," she said, holstering the weapon.

Tom wouldn't have been the first man she'd shot, but, hell! He was just a scared, sick, confused kid who was short on brains. He needed help, not a slug in his thigh. She started to chase after him, but stopped short at the clearing's edge. Racing through a swamp at night was not high on the list of sane activities. The kid would have to take his chances.

Anyway, she'd confiscated Tom's weapons and insured he'd harm no more animals under Parks Service protection. The crippled doe was recovering in the compound. She'd done her job. This was Sheriff Rudge's jurisdiction, and he was responsible for any escaped mental patients ...or would be after she told him about Tom Mason. She couldn't take care of the whole world.

Still, the ranger wished Tom had come quietly.

Cool air tickled the nape of her neck, left exposed by the tight braiding of her coarse black hair. She turned to retrieve the arrows before heading back to the ranger station, where she could stretch out on a cot for a couple of hours before Bill turned up. Hernandez was one of those fortunate few who needed comparatively little sleep—but she *had* to have that little. Otherwise she'd be crankier than usual, which was already enough for most of the people she knew.

Damn! On top of everything else, she hadn't had a chance to check on that reporter camping on Holroyd Hummock. The woman seemed competent, but even the most experienced outdoor folk ran into problems they couldn't handle. A part-time professional guide had vanished not three days ago, Rudge had told her. Hernandez didn't want to seem like a mother hen, but she couldn't help feeling some responsibility for the reporter. The ranger's own sightings had helped pinpoint Holroyd

Hummock as the best viewing site. Besides, Hernandez admitted, she was curious as to whether the reporter had found anything concrete, something that would explain just what the ranger, and others, really had seen.

Tomorrow for sure, she'd take the skiff to Holroyd.

Hernandez paused in the center of the clearing, poaching evidence in hand, and looked at the thick growth surrounding her. Above, stars in the eastern sky were starting to melt, but night's shadows still clung deep. She recalled again the huge, vague shape she'd thrice seen shambling through distant sawgrass.

If the Everglades night could fire the imagination of a down-to-earth woman like herself, Hernandez mused, small wonder that Tom Mason's mind was unhinged.

SIX

Blood growled low as he stepped into early morning sunlight at Miami International Airport. Instinctively, his left arm shot up to cover his exposed face. He forced it down. His gaunt, pale-skinned figure attracted too much attention as it was. He reached in his breast pocket for the dark glasses provided by Arthur Blanchard. They were better than nothing.

Sun could wither the vampire to dust in moments, but Blood was preserved by the subtlest of his transmutations; he'd taken on human form. Although the outward signs were minor—his fangs retracted, of course, and his eyes turned dark brown from feral red—the change was significant enough to let him shed the unique vulnerabilities of his kind. There were disadvantages because Blood also took on human frailties, and could be injured or slain by any number of conventional means, but those deaths lasted only until sunset.

Blood hurried into the shade of the terminal. There he paused to look back over the field. He did not bother with the long landing strips reserved for jets and passenger planes. It was on one of the shorter strips used by private aircraft that Blood would find his connection for the short hop to an airfield near Everglades City.

His gaze paused on a Cessna that was being unloaded under the directions of a stocky, olive-skinned man with close-cropped black hair. Despite the warm weather, the man wore a heavy, dark blue peacoat buttoned from top to bottom, but it was not the eccentric garb that held Blood's attention. Two thick-muscled men were sliding a rectangular crate out of the Cessna's cargo hold and onto a dolly. As they wheeled the box toward the open rear doors of a black Chevrolet van, Blood saw that it was almost large enough to substitute for the coffin-crate he'd traveled in during his early years as a vampire.

Blood felt a nostalgic pang for that crude transport, which had survived a crash landing on Dr. Bedloe's artificial island and the subsequent days of exposure to salt air and water. He no longer needed such a resting place, for it was discovered that prolonged suspended animation all but eliminated his need to rest while on assignment. Still, those six sides and the absolute darkness they provided had given him a sense of security in a way the living could never wholly understand.

Such reverie was a rare thing for Blood. He wished he had more opportunity to indulge in it. Random musings helped maintain a balance on that thin line between mortal and monster, allowing Blood to retain some bits of his humanity.

"Your name Cuardi?"

Blood turned to face a long-limbed black man in an orange aviator's jump suit. Although Blood was taller than average, and his cadaverous appearance gave the illusion of further height, he had to look up to meet the speaker's dark brown eyes.

"Al Cuardi. That's what they call me."

"That's my Piper Cub you've been admiring," the black man said, pointing past the Cessna. "I'm called Sandy."

Blood nodded, noticing the smaller airplane for the first time. Then he turned back to the man with the nut-brown skin and tight-curled, jet-black hair.

"Sandy?"

Sandy grinned. "The full handle is Sanders Charleston. Momma loved Paul Robeson, but I gave her a hard time getting born and she was a little confused. Instead of naming me after Robeson's character in 'Sanders of the River,' I was named for Leslie Banks's."

"Lucky she didn't call you Quartermain. "

Sandy's grin spread wider. "I do have a kid brother named Solomon," he admitted. "Anyway, your magazine wired that you needed a plane and pilot to fly you to Everglades city."

Blood nodded again. "Easier to rent a car, I suppose, but I dislike driving and my deadline...."

The roar of a departing jet drowned the rest of Blood's words. Sandy headed towards his Piper Cub with long, easy strides, goggles bouncing against his narrow chest. The vampire trotted to his side.

"You don't owe me any explanations," the pilot said when Blood had joined him. "I've been paid in advance, and that's all I need to know. Is that all your luggage, that flight bag? No typewriter case?"

Blanchard must have been upset, to miss that detail, but Blood hadn't missed it. "I dictate notes on a tape recorder and phone my story in, if necessary." Sandy shrugged, stopping abruptly alongside his plane. "That'll save time, then. I've already filed a standing flight plan, and we can take off as soon as I get the okay from the tower. There's a machine by the hangar if you'd like some coffee first."

Blood's expression was bland, but inwardly he grimaced at the thought of the thin, bitter liquid that was the only human sustenance he took, and then only when socially expedient. "I had something earlier."

"Then climb aboard and strap yourself in."

In the cockpit, Sandy was all business. Once they were airborne, the pilot spoke only to point out local landmarks. From two kilometers above the marshlands, there weren't many, but Blood took a professional interest. A vast scar in the Great Cypress Swamp stood out, revealing runways constructed for a proposed Jetport.

"That's where you would have landed, instead of Miami," Sandy explained, "if the conservationists hadn't stepped in."

Since the project's abandonment, the swamp was reclaiming its own, but decades would pass before those runways would be fully overgrown.

"If it had been built, you wouldn't be flying me now, would you?" Blood asked.

Charleston shrugged. "Swamp's fine the way it is, I think. I've got no beef with alligators."

SEVEN

Sheriff Paul Rudge resembled an animated scarecrow. Hair like bleached straw topped a face burnt red and leathery by years of Florida sun. Fifty-nine years old, Rudge looked closer to seventy, but moved like a man in his forties. He treated Blood's interest in the skunk-ape as a good-natured joke, but was willing to talk. His district was sparsely populated, and where there are few people there is little trouble. Search parties and hurricane relief formed the bulk of the sheriff s work. Answering a reporter's questions on a slow day was a welcome diversion.

"It's unusual to have a flap like this in the winter," Rudge explained, offering a thick file of reports for Blood's inspection. "I keep the sightings together. Reason they were handy, I had another reporter here last week asking about the same thing. What was her name? Blanker, Blankart...."

"Blanchard."

"That was it. Andrea Blanchard. Nice young lady. You know her?"

"By reputation. My editor told me the Examiner was working on this story as well."

Rudge nodded amiably. "Yep, people start seeing some kind of monster creeping around the swamp every year or two. Usually it's in the summer, when there's a lot of tourists who don't know what the hell they're looking at half the time. Word spreads, and for days afterwards everybody and their brother sees creatures behind every mangrove. Most folks don't realize how easily a man's eyes can fool him, especially at night. I had one deputy, bright boy, keen eyes, put a whole round of .38

shells into that cypress out front. He swore he saw a bear rearing up to attack him."

Blood dutifully copied names and addresses from the file in his soiled and dog-eared notebook, keeping up his reporter's pose. An air conditioner rattled in the window behind Rudge.

"I tend to agree, Sheriff. From the statements I see here, this skunk-ape seems to be another case of mass delusion. But my editor still wants the story. *Heaven and Earth* publishes the full facts on such anomalies, verified as completely and accurately as possible." Blood smiled wryly. "Which may be why we don't match the circulation of our competitors."

Rudge tilted his straight-back chair to balance on its rear legs. He scratched his furrowed neck. "Excuse an old cracker's philosophizing, but I don't see why people have to make up things to satisfy their imaginations. Seems to me there're enough real mysteries and wonders to confound a man."

"Exactly our position," Blood replied. He leaned forward, though not too close. Even in his human form, the agent gave off a faint, graveyard odor. The sheriff's office was small and enclosed, and the air conditioner could do only so much against Florida heat. "I've heard that Andrea Blanchard is a good reporter, but she's hamstrung by the Examiner editorial policy. A nothing story won't sell papers at the check-out counter. If she doesn't turn in something sensationalistic she'll be lucky to recover expenses."

Rudge's eyebrows crawled up his forehead. "She seemed sincere," he hedged.

Blood leapt to his feet, slapping the notebook on the edge of Rudge's desk. "You've given me an idea, Sheriff, that may keep my investigation from being a complete washout. If Ms. Blanchard is really good, she must hate working for that rag. *Heaven and Earth* is always looking for dependable staff writers. The pay will barely keep one in peanut butter sandwiches, but at least you can face yourself in the mirror." That is, Andrea could, he added silently.

"Well, I don't know about that," the sheriff replied. "She hasn't been seen for a while."

Blood looked dismayed. "Lost in the Everglades?"

"Not officially. Last I'd heard, she was camping out on Holroyd Hummock, where the ape's been sighted most often."

"Alone?"

Rudge sighed and nodded. "Independent type. As far as I know, though, she got disgusted and went home without telling anyone. I hope so. I didn't like the idea when I heard about it, but she'd already gotten her permit. Damned Yankees traipsing about in the muck as if they were on a city street ...! It's a wonder they don't all get sucked to the bottom of a quicksand patch." Rudge seemed oblivious of Blood's own northern accent.

"Is it difficult to track someone through the swamp?" he asked.

"Hell, yes. A fella could disappear in those bogs without a trace. Scavengers don't leave much. Sometimes we find 'em alive if they really want to be found and have an ounce of sense in their skulls. Sometimes we just find what's left. Too often, we have to close the file unsolved. Nothing else we can do, short of draining the entire 'glades." The sheriff peered at Blood through narrowed eyes. His mouth set into a scowl line. "I hope you don't plan anything stupid. If you want to go into the swamp, get a good guide. I can recommend a couple."

"I appreciate the offer. A colleague mentioned one name to me before I left: Frank Jordan. Is he any good?"

Rudge rubbed sweat from around his deep set eyes. He glanced at the air conditioner behind him. The fetid decaying odor of the surrounding marsh seemed stronger than usual today, even with the windows shut.

"Jordan's no good?" Blood continued.

"Oh, he's all right. Or was. Not a professional guide, but he'd help an occasional tourist for a consideration. Had a condo in Miami, but went hunting or fishing every other week. You'd think he'd've known the swamp like the back of his hand, at least the parts he hunted in. Doesn't matter. The land'll fool you. Changes with the tides and the season. Only takes a minute's carelessness."

"Would an experienced outdoorsman get lost?"

"Hell, I could get lost, and I was born and raised here. You can't plan for everything. He could've been bitten by a poisonous snake, or broken a leg. Of course, we should have found the body by now." Rudge shook his head.

"You couldn't have searched the whole swamp," said Blood.

"Nope, but we got a good idea where he vanished. We found his outboard. The county hauled a dredge to the area, but it didn't do much good. I'll show you the problem."

Rudd stood up and pressed a gnarled finger against a map of lower Florida taped to the rough-paneled wall behind his desk, to the left of the air conditioner. The fingertip circled an area three kilometers outside the border of the National Park.

"This section's called the Loop," Rudge said. "And all this here is bog. When the tide is up the soft ground extends even further. Some of it is thin mud; a man can stay afloat for twenty minutes if he doesn't thrash around. Other parts'll suck you down in no time flat."

"A bottomless pit," Blood said.

"Ain't no such thing," Rudge snapped. "We just can't reach the bottom for one reason or another. Some of the holes bypass the 'glades altogether and drain into the Gulf. A body caught in one of those may wash up on shore in Mexico or Louisiana."

"I take it," Blood said, "you've given up the search for Jordan?"

Rudge sighed. "As of yesterday. If he hasn't shown up by now, he's not going to, and no next of kin has been nagging us for the body."

Blood studied the map trying to soak up all its topographical detail. He wished that vampires possessed photographic memories. Blood had to rely on years-old training, since refresher courses were out of the question for him.

The vampire's long, thin finger traced a path from the location of Jordan's abandoned outboard to the hummock on which Andrea Blanchard had camped. Less than a kilometer.

Blood noticed Rudge studying him closely. He flashed a quick grin. "This section looks solid."

"Doesn't it, though? At low tide you can walk most of it. This area here was once used for farming, but hurricanes kept wiping out the crops and destroying the topsoil. Now there're just a few marginal orange-growers to the north here. That's

Holroyd Hummock your thumb is on. Not strictly an island any more except when the tide's up, four or five hours out of every twenty-four."

Keeping his eyes on the map, Blood asked, "When's the next low tide?"

Rudge looked at his watch. "Let's see, the time now is ... hell, it's past twelve! I've gabbed away a whole morning with you, and I still have to make my rounds. Next low tide won't be until before midnight."

Blood nodded and stepped back from the map.

"I don't advise going into the swamp at night even with a guide," Rudge warned. "Wait for morning to nose around. You're determined to look for that damned skunk-ape, are you?"

Blood spread his hands, palms up. "That's what I'm here for. I have to go through the motions, and file a story even if there is no story."

"Well, don't worry about the tides. The best way to reach Holroyd is by boat, from the south. Looks roundabout, but it's faster than tramping through all that muck. I know; I've done both."

"I'll remember that. I thank you for your time and advice, Sheriff."

"You'd better keep out of the sun, too. Skin as pale as yours'll fry crimson in fifteen minutes."

"Fortunately, I'm a night person."

"And if I were you, I'd stop at the ranger station to chat with Lucy Hernandez."

Blood halted at the door and glanced at the file on Rudge's desk. "The same Hernandez who reported three sightings ...?"

"The same, but there's a better reason to talk to her. She's an expert on local history. She also issued the permit to that lady reporter. She can tell you all kinds of things I can't if you handle her the right way."

"Which way is that?"

Rudge let out a deep laugh. "If you find out, let me know."

EIGHT

Robert stopped in front of the door to room seventeen and tucked his dark green T-shirt into the waistband of his jeans. His rubber soles scraped nervously on the pebbled cement walk, but his green eyes glittered and his tanned cheeks puffed out with the smug pride of a royal favorite bringing good news to his king. And why not? Robert was three weeks short of his twentieth birthday, and had only joined the Free Thought Alliance this past summer. Almost any other member of the Alliance was better qualified, in terms of age, experience, and seniority, but he had been selected by Snow to take Sleet's place as executive aide.

Full of the importance of his new position, Robert turned to survey the motel's motor court. All clear, as he'd expected. He didn't complete the scan, for his eyes met those of the olive-skinned man in the buttoned-up peacoat who waited in the deepest shade of the overhang of the rooms on the opposite side of the court. They were the eyes of a man who does not like to be kept waiting in the open; a man whose soft voice could make a simple greeting sound threatening.

Robert spun around and rapped out the day's code: two-three-one.

"Enter," came the muffled reply.

Robert pushed the door inward. All lights were off, and the shades were drawn, so that the reflection of the sun from a dozen windshields behind Robert brightened the room noticeably. The young man shut the door at once.

A dark form lay on the furthest of the twin beds, betrayed in the gloom by clean white gauze dressings. This figure glanced at Robert, stiffened at the flash of light that had accompanied his entrance, and then settled down again.

Robert looked at the short, rotund, pale-skinned man sitting by the dressing table with thick, short-fingered hands folded over an expanse of yellow terrycloth robe. "Cap'n Gray is here, sir."

The fat man turned ice-blue eyes on Robert. His lips twisted in contrived bemusement. "What is your name?"

The boy's cheek twitched, as though he'd been slapped. Forgotten the name of his new aide? Surely not!

"It's Robert, sir," he answered with a dry mouth.

"Robert. I thought so." The seated man stared abruptly into the mirror, as if distracted by some motion there. Slowly his attention returned to his aide, though the eyes kept darting back, reluctant to abandon their suspicions.

"How did you feel when I asked for your name?"

Robert shifted his weight from one foot to the other. "I don't know. It seemed odd...."

"Shocked? Amazed? Dismayed? That the leader of the Free Thought Alliance could not recall who his new second in command was?"

"I never doubted...."

"Imagine how *I* felt, then, that you'd forgotten *my* name."

Sweat beaded on Robert's brow. The room's air conditioner was broken. "I never...."

"How long have you been with the Alliance, Robert?"

"About four months. But in my heart I've always...."

"Four months. Of course, until the last day or so we've exchanged few words, but that is still enough time, I'd think, for you to learn that my name is not Sir. I call myself Snow, Robert. Snow. I chose that name for a reason. As leader of this Alliance, I must be more than a man; I must be a symbol, an affirmation of our organization's ideals. Like the snow, we will purify the world of its materialistic philosophies so we can bring about a rebirth of harmony and accord. Remember that, Robert. Snow. Use that name when you address me. Every time. Circuitous salutations are suspect, and can harbor treacherous attitudes."

"Yes, s ... Snow."

Robert licked his lips. The piercing gaze of Snow's icy pupils seemed all the more intense in contrast with the milky flesh of his face, and his pale, baby-soft hair. Robert was struck once again by the realization that this deceptively fragile man was capable of having him killed at the slightest hint of disloyalty. Robert already knew, had convinced himself, that he would sacrifice his own life if Snow told him it was necessary.

"Practice it, Robert. The name must come easily to your tongue. I will overlook your indiscretion this time. Send in Cap'n Gray."

Robert lowered his head and backed out of the room. He could not face Snow's glare.

When he had gone, the figure on the bed spoke.

"You are hard on him, my friend. Have you forgotten how it was when we started? The mistakes we made!" The man looked at the bandages at the ends of his arms and added, bitterly, "The mistakes we still make!"

Snow scowled. "If we are to succeed, I must have unquestioning obedience, even to my smallest whim. I've tightened discipline in the months you were away. We cannot afford dissension. In a way, it is fortunate that Sleet was killed. He was beginning to impinge on my authority. Robert will serve my needs better, I think. I can mold him to my ways." Snow leaned forward, peering into the shadows. "Or have you ambitions of your own at stake?"

The reply came as a sour laugh. "I cannot even feed myself, unless I eat like an animal. How could I wrest control from you? You need not fear me, Snow, nor Robert, nor Sleet if he still lived. Beware of private demons; they are the stuff of a man's destruction. I learned that much in prison."

Snow smiled grimly. "It's the demons now controlling the world that I intend to vanquish."

The door opened again, less surely. Robert guided Cap'n Gray within, and retired wordlessly.

The stocky Cap'n stood before Snow with his hands sunk deep in the pockets of his peacoat. With his taut, hard-muscled frame, close-cropped jet black hair, swarthy complexion and dashing pencil-thin mustache, Gray was physically as opposite from the Alliance leader as could be imagined.

"Where is my merchandise?" Snow demanded. No amenities, no words of greeting, no handshakes. Gray did not even take his hands from his pockets. These two had done business many times, and social graces were no part of their agreement.

"The crate is in the back of a rented Chevy van," drawled Cap'n Gray. "It's parked a kilometer down the highway. I'm sure I wasn't followed, but I did have the sensation of being watched at Miami Airport."

"The order is complete?"

"Almost."

Snow's blue eyes burned with anger. "You let me down?"

Gray seemed unperturbed. "I did the best I could in the little time you gave me. Your coded cable made up quite a shopping list. Brownings, M16s, sniper rifles, all unregistered military weapons, many never fired before. Quality merchandise, and ammunition in quantity to match. I even threw in some extra rounds for your own M3A1, to compensate for the shortage of M16s. What are you up to, anyway? Re-tooling your whole organization? Or did you just complete a successful recruitment drive?"

"That," snarled Snow, "is not your concern."

Cap'n Gray shook his head. He lowered himself to sit at the foot of the unoccupied bed and leaned forward. His hands never left the pockets.

"I'm afraid it is very much my concern. If too many unregistered weapons fall into the wrong hands at once, you'll have treasury agents poking around, complicating business. That would be a bad thing for both of us."

Snow closed his pop-eyes and sat back heavily. The motel chair creaked under his weight. Snow pursed his lips in and out, fishlike, as he debated himself. After a moment, the eyes bulged open again.

"All right, Cap'n. The circumstances are embarrassing, but I can assure you neither of us is in danger of discovery."

"That's fine. I like being reassured. Go on."

Snow lowered his voice until it was barely audible. "The bulk of our arsenal was in a camper we'd bought in Jacksonville.

One of our men was assigned to drive this vehicle to a selected safe haven in the Great Cypress Swamp. He took a wrong turn."

"Where are those guns now?"

"Still in the camper, at the bottom of a pool of quicksand. We had only an assortment of small arms left, and of course my own machine gun, which I always keep with me. Normally we would have simply laid low for a few weeks, but we'd already taken certain irreversible steps that *are* outside your concern. Half my force was sent on fund-raising expeditions along the Gold Coast, and I cabled you at once."

Gray nodded thoughtfully. "I wouldn't have cared to be in your driver's shoes. Or did he go down with the ship?"

"Oh, he survived." Snow's lips twisted into a mocking smile. "For several hours."

The Cap'n grimaced. "No details, please. I haven't your stomach for it. Let's see the money."

Snow opened the drawer of the dressing table and removed a flat metal box. He hefted it in one swollen hand. His eyes narrowed as he faced Gray again.

"I'm not sure you're entitled to the full sum. You admit the order is incomplete, and there's the question of late delivery. My cable stressed urgency."

Gray shrugged, keeping his eyes on the cash box. "It took time to arrange for the airplane. An extra expense I'm absorbing since it was entailed for my safety, not yours."

"You should have come by boat, as usual."

"I had a run-in with the Coast Guard in Gulf waters earlier this year. They didn't get a good description, but some of those laddies have sharp memories."

Snow grunted. "Yours is a risky business, but it was your choice."

"And when it gets too risky, I'll choose retirement as a wealthy man. Until then, if you wish to use my services in the future, I must insist on payment in full." At last, Gray removed a hand from his coat pocket, to accept the metal box.

"Count it, if you like," Snow offered.

"At my leisure. You know what would happen if it came up short, so I'm sure you've already checked the amount. Here's the

key to the van." Gray placed the key on the bed as he stood up.
"Have someone drop it off at an agency lot. I paid for the day's
rental in advance. There's a ride waiting for me already."

Snow's lip curled. He didn't like taking orders. "It'll be taken
care of."

Gray nodded and stepped to the door. He paused with his left
hand on the doorknob, the cashbox under his right arm. His head
inclined slightly toward the man in the bed.

"I hope you're keeping your friend under close wraps."

The man on the bed swung his feet onto the thin carpeting. He
started to rise, his eye glaring with menace.

"Stay there!" Snow snapped; then, to Gray: "We know what
we're doing."

"I hope so. Every law enforcement agency east of the Mississippi
is looking for him. Still, the government believes he's left the States
altogether, so you might get away with it."

Snow watched Cap'n Gray leave, and stared at the closed door
for a long moment afterward. His lips pursed in thought.

The man on the bed glowered silently, digging his wrist stumps
into the bedsheets, in frustration. Finally, his rage boiled over.

"He knew! He knew who I was! I'd never met him! How could
he know? Who told him? Robert?"

Snow hissed with ill-concealed irritation. "Calm yourself,
Rodicio. Even Robert would not be that foolish. With your bandaged wrists, and that patch over your right eye socket, you are
hardly inconspicuous. The Alliance has dealt with Cap'n Gray
many times. He knows that we do not travel with members so
badly injured; they could prove liabilities. Only one man is important enough for us to break that rule, and that man is you: the noto-
rious Rodicio Chavez."

"But he knows! He will tell! The reward money! We must stop
him!" Spittle flecked Rodicio's lips.

Snow's face suffused with pink. "And you speak to me of private demons! Cap'n Gray will keep your secret. The reward for
your capture is little more than the reward for *any* information
regarding the Free Thought Alliance, and considerably less than
his profit on our recent transaction. It could not compensate for the
punishment that would be his should his gun-running activities

come to light, as of course they would."

"He could make a deal. Have his charges dropped."

Snow shook his head. "Gray is not so trusting. He also knows that we, or his other customers, would take revenge."

Chavez threw himself back on the bed. He glared angrily at the peeling ceiling, daring the roof to cave in. "We should have killed him."

Snow laughed. "We never had the chance, Rodicio. You heard him. He had a ride waiting. Do you think he told us that to be pleasant? Believe me, if Cap'n Gray had not left the room when he did, if we'd delayed him but a few more minutes, *we* would be in no position to enjoy his silence. Don't look so glum, my friend; this is the way we must work. Trust between two parties can only be assured when each possesses equal force. That is why we fight, to destroy *their* power so that the world may operate on trust again."

Rodicio raised his arms over his head. "If only I had my hands again! I could have strangled my name on his tongue."

Snow slapped a heavy hand on the dressing table. "He never said your name. That was his way of telling us he would not talk."

Chavez crossed his arms over his chest. He took a deep breath, and let it out slowly. "All right, Snow, you win. I would not have strangled Cap'n Gray. But to be able to!"

Snow ran a pudgy hand through his fine, soft hair. "Perhaps you should have stayed in that hospital until the prostheses were attached."

Rodicio made a rude noise. "Yes, I'm sure they'd have been happy to let me escape then!" In a lower tone, he added, "Metal claws are a poor substitute for flesh and sinew, anyway." He turned to face the wall.

Snow heaved up his bulk and walked to the side of the bed. He gripped Chavez's shoulder in comradeship. The maimed man was shaking beneath Snow's thick fingers.

"You will be avenged, my friend," Snow said. "That is our purpose in having captured Blanchard's daughter. Trust me."

"I apologize for my outburst," Chavez said, his voice muffled by pillows. "Of course I trust you, Snow."

Snow released his grip and stood over his crippled comrade. That might be your next mistake, he mused.

NINE

Swish! Thuck!

The machete slashed through a clump of Spanish moss and bit into one of the pillars supporting the veranda roof. The dark-haired woman with skin the color of whole wheat bread made a sour face and yanked her blade free. A chip of graying wood flew from the pillar and vanished into the surrounding brush. It left a pale yellow scar. There were many such scars on this pillar and its fellows, as well as on the railing and even the eave.

The dislodged greenery landed on her boot, and she kicked it off through a gap in the railing. With her sleeve, she wiped perspiration from forehead and upper lip. Then she tugged at her uniform's blouse, where it clung to her skin. The afternoon seemed unseasonably warm. She considered taking a quick dip in the stream that ran behind the cabin.

Blood clambered up the veranda steps. The steps creaked, even under his light tread; but he wasn't trying for stealth.

The woman turned to chop away another strand of encroaching nature, pointedly ignoring the ashen-faced newcomer. Let him talk to her assistant inside the station. Bill was better at dealing with the public than she was, especially today. She kept brooding over the poacher who'd gotten away in the early hours of morning.

Blood opened the screen door. Boards groaned and rattled under his scuffling feet. His noisome presence demanded her attention. Her lips formed a thin straight line, and the jaw muscles tightened.

"Lucille Hernandez?"

The machete claimed another vegetative victim before Hernandez turned to face the lean stranger with the sleek black hair and compelling, reddish-brown eyes. Her own frame was spare, but more compact; every pound counted. She pushed a thick lock of reddish-black hair behind her ear.

"I'm *Ranger* Hernandez, yes. What are you?"

Blood had his press card in hand. "Al Cuardi, of *Heaven and Earth* magazine. We're doing a feature on the skunk-ape alleged to be roaming these parts. I'm told you can help me."

"You've been told wrong. There's no such thing." The machete flashed again in the afternoon sun.

"Sheriff Rudge said you'd reported seeing the creature."

"He did, eh? Well, Paul gets so many calls from kooks he sometimes forgets who told him what."

"I've seen the reports. Three of them. I don't know for a fact that it was your signature at the bottom, but I can find out."

The broad blade missed a matted cluster of stems and sank deep into a pillar. The railing quivered as Hernandez freed the knife. "All right, I saw something. The local paper called it a skunk-ape; I didn't."

"What did you call it?"

"Don't know. Don't care."

"Speculate. An expert's opinion."

Hernandez licked her lips, tasting salt. "If it'll get rid of you. I'd guess it was an overgrown 'gator or croc' with a notion to lean up along a tree trunk. They keep growing, you know; the older, the bigger. There must be alligators over two hundred years old, in parts of the 'glades no one will ever see. Unless of course we destroy the whole system and turn the swamp into a Sahara desert." She jabbed the point of her knife at the surrounding underbrush.

"Is that all? And you thought it worth reporting to the sheriff's office?"

"If you don't like it, go back to your air-conditioned hotel room on the Gold Coast and make up your own story. That's what you people do anyway." She shrugged without looking at him.

The agent resisted an urge to grasp the woman's shoulders

and spin her around. It would take but a few seconds: the turn, his glare, the glazing over of her eyes as she submitted to his will. She would readily answer his questions then.

Or would she? Hernandez was headstrong and clever. None could resist Blood's hypnotic powers at night, when his vampiric abilities peaked. By day, however, a strong personality could withstand him and, forewarned, could deny him a second chance.

He tried another tack.

"I've run into your attitude before, Ranger Hernandez. Let me tell you that *Heaven and Earth* has a reputation for honesty and thorough investigation of anomalies such as your skunk-ape. If we uncover a fraud, we won't bury the story or play along. Last month we exposed that couple in Missouri who'd claimed to hear Jimmy Hoffa speaking from a flying saucer. In July, we ran a long article on the Texas faith healer who'd said he was in Tibet during the six years he spent in a federal prison for mail fraud. We make up nothing, Ranger. We are not to be classed with the Weekly Examiner and its ilk."

Hernandez glared at him, eyes flashing. Blood had struck a nerve.

"Just what the hell do you want, Cuardi?"

"I'd like to see the spot where you saw your ...'gator."

"No way. I've wasted enough time with you. I spent most of last night patching up a deer and tracking a scared-witless kid through the swamp. There's three months' worth of paperwork on my desk, just covering routine Park duties, and in my so-called free time I'm pushing to get part of the Great Cypress turned into a national preserve."

"You're not doing paperwork now."

"Because I won't spend the whole day wearing out my tail behind a desk. That isn't why I applied for this job. And *this* has to be done, too. If I didn't cut back, the swamp would cover this place in a month."

"I wouldn't want that to happen. Continue your pruning."

"I intend to."

"I promise to stay out of your way while you tell me about Ben Holroyd's plantation."

Hernandez wrinkled her nose. "The ruins on Holroyd Hummock? What for?"

"You saw whatever you saw in that area, according to the reports. Three times."

"What I say three times is true?" She swatted at a mosquito hovering by her left ear. Her visitor seemed unbothered by insects, almost as if they shunned him, which did not improve her disposition. "You already know all the answers, it seems. Go away and stay there."

Blood leaned forward, resting his hand on the unsteady railing beside the ranger. If she was defying him to apply pressure, he would oblige.

"Original sources are the most valuable assets of a good reporter, Ranger Hernandez. I hope you won't force me to go over your head. Government administrators tend to overreact when a member of the fourth estate complains of uncooperativeness. The slightest hint of unfavorable publicity throws them into fits." Blood's smile, rarely pleasant, was certainly not so now. "Of course, it would be unethical of me to let such pettiness color my reporting, but certain types of people don't understand about scruples...."

The machete hissed through the air and buried itself half a centimeter into the railing, close enough to have given the agent a manicure if he'd needed one. Blood did not move his hand.

"You bastard," the ranger spat. "And Rafferty *would* make a nuisance of himself, too."

"I thought you'd come around."

"I can't tell you a damned thing you can't find in a local history book."

"The nearest library is fifty kilometers from here. You're not. Aren't you supposed to provide information to visitors?"

Leaving the machete in place, Hernandez grasped a pillar, ignoring the splinters that dug into her roughed palms. She swung her body up and around, landing lightly on the railing. Slight as she was, the balustrade creaked under her weight. Blood moved to join her perch.

"I wouldn't do that," she warned gleefully. "Wood's a bit rotten. It barely supports me. We've been meaning to replace it, but what with all the interruptions...."

The veranda was bare of furniture, or even a crate Blood could pull over. He shrugged and stood where he was. The scowl on his face was for the ranger's benefit; beneath it, he was amused. Hernandez had perhaps earned this concession. It cost him nothing to make her victory appear greater than it was, and she might speak more freely.

"In 1813," the ranger began, "a Scotsman named Zepaniah Kingsley settled near present-day St. Augustine and set himself up as a slave trader, importing slaves into the United States had been prohibited since 1808," she continued, "but Florida was not then part of the Union. Slaves were easily smuggled across the Georgia border, and not by Kingsley alone.

"Kingsley stood out among his fellow slavers, however, in his scorn for the debasing system of dragging the survivors of a cramped, unhealthy ocean voyage to the auction block for immediate sale to the highest bidder. When Kingsley bought slaves, he taught them farm skills and handicrafts and how to survive in their new world. This increased the slaves' values by as much as fifty percent when he resold them to plantation owners in Georgia and the Carolinas, and during the training he had free labor for the less profitable business of growing cotton and vegetables. Kingsley also kept his slaves in family units, and gave each family its own small cabin and a piece of land to work for themselves. He even married Ann Jai, the daughter of an African chieftain, although neither she nor any of her children were ever permitted to live in the main house.

"In the 1820's, Florida became a United States territory, and Kingsley ceased his trading activities. However, one of his foremen, Ben Holroyd, left to continue the business among the twisting rivers of the Great Cypress Swamp. On the hummock that later bore his name, Holroyd established a smaller, cruder, and far less humane version of Kingsley's operation.

"Holroyd believed in fast turnover. The longer it took to sell a slave, the more chance there was of getting caught. He eliminated the training program and kept most of the slaves prisoners in a long barracks. A handful were forced to do the work of three times their number to keep the plantation self-sufficient.

"It didn't work. Many shipments were intercepted by the pirates then terrorizing the coastal waters or by the U.S. Navy, which had a base at Key West to deal with those pirates. The human cargo that did arrive could not work the land efficiently enough to even feed themselves. Furthermore, General Andrew Jackson, governor of the new territory, was harassing the native Seminoles, and they in turn took it out on whoever was handy. Many slaves were killed or escaped during Seminole attacks. More succumbed to malaria and starvation. In less than a year, Holroyd abandoned the hummock. The Seminoles burnt the plantation to the ground the day he left, and only the sturdy slave quarters remained standing, though badly damaged.

"That enough for you?" the ranger concluded. She was pleased to hear the veranda boards creak as Blood shifted from one foot to the next.

"Perhaps," Blood said. He shut his notebook so that she could not peer at the meaningless scratches he'd made during her lecture. "I'll let you know. My editor likes lots of background … gives a nice selection of sidebar material."

"I'm thrilled for you."

"So when do you take me to this Holroyd Hummock?"

Hernandez leapt from her perch, freeing her machete in the same motion. The railing shivered perilously. She glared up at him, her nose wrinkled at his fetid breath, her eyes bubbling pools of oil. "You never let up, do you?"

Blood inclined his head, accepting the compliment. "Sheriff Rudge said I needed a good guide. I suspect you're the best."

The ranger scowled. "I'm pretty good, but Yankee flattery won't work on me. There are others just as good, and far more willing to be a padded item on your expense account. I've got too much work around here to take off on a wild goose chase, especially for someone else's goose, and it's too late in the day for it anyway."

"Of course," he said softly. "I can see that."

The sudden reasonableness of his tone surprised Hernandez. "You can?"

"I'm not a monster, Ranger Hernandez." He shrugged. "Not completely. I'll come back tomorrow for the tour." Blood gave her an informal salute, turned smartly on one heel, and started toward the veranda steps.

Blood did not really need a guide, and would more likely find one a hindrance, but Hernandez didn't have to know that. Since he was prepared to concede on that point, he could use it to negotiate for further information, if necessary.

The ranger's face darkened. She glared balefully at the agent's back. The stinging reply she wanted would not come; only a hiss escaped her drawn-tight lips. Speech was beyond her.

She tightened her grip on the machete's black taped handle, and attacked another clump of intruding vegetation. The Spanish moss was in big trouble now.

At the foot of the steps, Blood paused to look back. "Try not to chop down the station," he called. Then he vanished down the trail.

Hernandez threw down her knife and stalked to the station's screen door. With any luck, Bill had made a fresh pot of coffee. Better yet, maybe he'd just reheated the vile stuff from that morning. It would suit her mood just fine.

TEN

As he stepped from the steamy bathroom of Room Seventeen, Robert was keenly aware of Snow's eyes following his movements. A dim lamp dispelled the twilight gloom. The Alliance leader beckoned the young man to his side. "I still hear water running," said Snow.

"He sent me out before the tub was full. Said he'd turn off the faucet with his toes." Robert smiled nervously. "He was like that when we helped him escape; kept wanting to do things himself."

"Maybe he'll drown himself," Snow muttered hopefully.

Robert's eyes dilated. "Snow?"

"Hm? Ah. I was just speculating about how difficult it must be for a man with Rodicio's pride to live with such losses. I'd probably drown myself. But he is, as we know, made of sterner stuff."

"Very much so," Robert replied reverently.

"Yes. Well. I have a job for you, Robert. Pick four men, one of whom will stay here to assist our noble comrade as necessary."

"Yes, Snow. And the other three?"

"Hm?"

"The other three. If I know what they're to do, I'll have a better idea of who to pick."

"The others will accompany us tonight."

"Us?"

"Yes. I'm giving you a chance to redeem yourself."

Robert licked his lips. "What should they prepare for?"

"We're going fishing."

"I don't understand."

Snow clasped his hands beneath his chin. Seated as he was, with the light at his back, his head seemed to rest on an under-inflated soccer ball. "With the help of Cap'n Gray, we can now investigate the deaths of our colleagues, the escape of our hostage, and the disappearances of Tom and Micky. The latter is not so important. Those two are either dead or traitors to our cause, which ultimately amounts to the same thing."

"We've all been eager for this, Snow."

Snow's face flushed coral. In the dim light, this was barely noticeable. "When I think that we had the man responsible for the Cleveland fiasco on his knees, ready at a word to free comrades and provide weapons for our noble cause … !" His breathing took on an unhealthy rasp.

Robert shuffled nervously to the door of the motel room. He did not care to witness Snow's temper unleashed. He'd seen what had happened to the driver who'd lost their arsenal. "I'll select the men immediately, Snow."

Snow nodded absently, then stopped him with a word. "Wait."

Robert's T-shirt grew clammy where it clung to his back. "Yes, Snow?"

"Select two men. The third shall be Farmer. He'll know best what I want, and how to get it."

Color drained from Robert's face. "But Farmer's our tor … our interrogation expert."

Snow pursed his lips in a smug smile. "Exactly. While we've cooled our heels in cheap motel rooms, the local police are likely looking into a routine disappearance. Pity the local force is too small for us to infiltrate, but the lack of publicity indicates they've either found nothing … or something significant. For us to cover the same ground would be not only time consuming but danger-ous. We'll take the direct route and see what this Sheriff Rudge knows."

Robert wiped damp palms on his jeans. "Won't Rudge be even more curious … and dangerous?"

Snow's ice-blue eyes fixed on Robert's. The youth looked down at his sneakers. "Now *you're* asking dangerous questions, Robert. Dangerous to yourself. Perhaps I am making a mistake in giving you this opportunity?"

"Please, s … Snow. I didn't mean …"

"A leader cannot afford mistakes."

Robert's knees grew weak. A dark stain spread on the left leg of his jeans, fortunately invisible in the poor light. He swallowed hard and managed to whisper, "I'm sorry, Snow. It's only that I don't wish to screw up because of something I don't know."

"Don't you trust Snow to tell you everything you need to know?"

"Of course I do."

"Then show your trust. Use your brain, as well. Naturally Rudge will be suspicious. That won't matter. By the time we have learned everything we can from him, with Farmer's aid, Sheriff Rudge will be in no condition to tell anyone else of those suspicions." Snow lurched to his feet. "We leave within the hour."

ELEVEN

On silent paws, Blood padded through tall, thick sawgrass. His snout wrinkled at the pervading odor of rotting flesh and vegetation, and his pointed ears twitched at every sound. No cricket's chirp, no frog's croaking, no distant roar of a bull alligator escaped his notice.

Lice crawled onto his thick gray fur, eagerly exploring new territory. They dropped off quickly. There was no nourishment on this wolf's shape for ordinary parasites. Blood was the parasite supreme.

Dense fog swirled through the swamp, or he'd have glided through the fetid air on batwings. A vampire's influence over the elements was overrated. Conditions had to be favorable to start with. Blood could dispel fog over a modest area, but he couldn't clear the entire swamp. Even now, eyes close to the ground, he found his keen night vision badly limited by the churning mist.

The circuitous northern route had cost him much time, but he'd been forced to take it. Several streams did not drain completely when the tide ebbed. These blocked Blood more effectively than a brick wall, which his inhuman strength could at least batter down. The vampire could not, in any landbound form, cross running water of his own volition. To transform into a bat or a mist each time he came to such a barrier was wearying. Transmutations made Blood thirsty, and the satiating effects of the canisters he'd drained in the cryogenic room wore off all too soon as it was. Fortunately, the restriction did not apply to standing pools or trickles less than a finger thick.

Now, at last, he should be near the spot where Frank Jordan's dinghy was found. If the map in Sheriff Rudge's office was accurate. If Blood recalled it correctly. If the shifting currents of the Great Cypress Swamp had not led his sense of direction astray. The boat was long gone, hauled away by the county, but there! A heap of mud along a river bank showed that dredging had been done within the last few days.

The wolf shape shimmered in the feeble moonlight that sifted through the canopy formed by cypress and mangrove. Blood rose up on his hind legs, stretching, stretching …. Hip joints shifted to permit bi-pedalism. Nails shrank back, and fingers curled forward where foretoes had been. The extended snout flattened as if crushed, and gray fur turned to fiber. In seconds, Blood had regained his vampiric aspect. His beige safari jacket flapped open, revealing the crimson inner lining.

With a gesture, the vampire dispersed the fog for a radius of three meters. He knelt to scrutinize the ground. Moving in a crouch, he slowly approached the cypress stand on the bank of the stream.

A growl of disappointment rose in his throat. Blood could usually count on finding clues that the keenest human would not spot. Here, time had eliminated what the rescue party hadn't already destroyed. Trampled grass sprang back or remained buried under muck. Threads were blown away or claimed for nesting material. Voracious insects devoured bloodstains.

Blood grimaced. He could not yet play the lone hand he favored. He still needed help from Rudge and Hernandez.

Tendrils of mist seeped into the cleared circle with Blood's consent. He turned from the bank, still in a crouch, prepared to resume his lupine form.

Two eyes, round with terror, watched from the brush ahead. They disappeared a second later, behind a gnarled cypress trunk.

Blood turned his head slowly from side to side, as though still searching, as though he had not spied the watcher; but he kept the cypress in sight. A moment later, he sighed aloud and stood erect. Mud squelched under his thick-soled boots. He walked hesitantly, this way and that, head bent to examine the ground. The path was not direct, but every step brought him closer to the tree.

The watcher dared not move.

The agent drew near enough to hear the other's ragged, heavy breathing. When they were ten meters apart, Blood smelled the growing fear. At four meters, the lurker's pulse throbbed at the limits of his hearing. A flight reaction was imminent.

Blood leapt, crashing through the brush. Hands reached forward to grasp clothing or flesh.

In panic, the watcher threw himself at his attacker.

Blood twisted in mid-leap, avoiding the brunt of impact. His right hand smashed into the watcher's abdomen. There was a rush of expelled air, a stifled moan, and a great thrashing as the man landed on his back in the mud.

Blood stared down at his prize. The man was young, perhaps barely out of his twenties. Khaki rags hung loosely on his slight frame. The fetid odor of the swamp clung to him, and his thick hair was clotted with filth. Face and clothing were also foully encrusted.

Blood hoped he'd not misjudged his blow and killed the man. He himself had survived point-blank gunshots, mortal knife wounds, and similar annoyances. The living were more fragile. It was easy to forget that.

The man moaned and drew up his knees, holding them against his chest with his arms. His head bent forward, eyes tightly shut. He rocked on his spine.

Blood rapped a kneecap sharply. The legs shot out straight. The young man's eyes flew open to glisten in the scattering of dim moonlight.

"Don't kill me!" he shrieked. "Please don't kill me! It wasn't my fault! It was that thing! It took them! It killed the others!"

Blood's icy grip closed on the youth's shoulder. The agent hauled him to his feet and held him upright against the cypress. Cowardice disgusted him. Blood knew what death was like. There *were* worse fates.

"Tell me your name."

The prisoner blubbered. Blood's free hand grabbed him under the chin to hold the head steady.

"Your name," he repeated.

"T-T-Tom."

"The rest of it."

"Tom. Tom tom. Tom tom tom tom tom tom...."

Blood released his hold and slapped him, raising a red mark on the right cheek. Tom's head moved with the blow, and he tried to bury his face against his left shoulder. He began sniffling.

Blood scowled. Tom was on the edge of a mental breakdown. There was no point in hypnotizing him. Tom was already too suggestible; controlling his will would not make him more coherent. Blood would have to let him ramble, guiding him as best he could, if he was to get any information out of him.

The vampire forced Tom's head up again. His voice was calm, deliberate, and imperious. "What are you doing here?"

"Hiding."

"From whom?"

"That thing ... Snow ... hide ... don't let it get me! It got Micky ... killed Sleet and the rest ... took the girl...."

Blood's grip on Tom's shoulder tightened. "What girl?"

"The girl. You know."

"What girl, Tom?"

"She was ... her father was going to get our comrades out of jail ... out of Cleveland. It took her ... took Micky ... all gone ... all dead ... thought I was dead ... maybe I am . ..." He slumped against the tree.

The agent's scowl deepened. If the fragments of Tom's story weren't just fantasy, Blood had gotten the break he was looking for. He'd found a member of the Free Thought Alliance—but too late. Tom seemed to be saying that the FTA no longer held Andrea Blanchard.

"Show me, Tom. Show me where this happened."

"No! *It* might be there! Snow might be there! Cops might be there! Never. Won't go back. Tried to. Wanted Sleet's rifle. To hunt. *It* was there. Waiting. Arrows no good. Ran away. Hungry. Can't let it get me. Rather starve. Won't let it kill me!" He met Blood's gaze for the first time. "You have food?"

"Take me to where this happened, Tom, or I'll kill you here and now." Tom licked his lips. He recognized the look on Blood's face. He'd seen the same look on Snow's, often enough.

"Don't let them kill me," he pleaded.

"I won't. No one else will touch you." But Blood could not include himself in that promise. He felt a burning tingle in the back of his throat. The thirst was building again.

TWELVE

Senator Rudolph Hastings stood before his liquor cabinet and poured two fingers of bourbon. He downed it neat, relishing the burning sensation in his throat, feeling the warmth spread up his wrinkled cheeks and past his tonsure of gray, thinning hair. He poured a second shot, took a slow sip, and turned. Now he was ready, if not willing, to face his late night visitor.

"Nice of you to finally get in touch with me, Allen," the senator rasped. Allen Davies slouched in the maroon lounge chair, grinned broadly, highlighting the square shape of his clean-cut jaw. He wore a powder-blue jogging suit and a matching terry-cloth headband. His yellow-striped Adidas dripped a dark, wet pool on the thick-piled carpet. His footprints could be traced all the way back to the entrance hall.

"Hey, no problem," Davies said. "What's a family for, right? Say, isn't your thermostat set a little high? We're supposed to conserve energy this winter." He unzipped the suit down to his ribs, exposing a thick mat of dark chest hair. A shark's tooth gleamed on the end of a thin chain.

Hastings took a long sip. "If you hadn't jogged two miles through the Washington snow, you wouldn't feel overheated. Don't change the subject. I've been trying to reach you for two days."

"Yes, and you used up half the tape on my answering machine. Very redundant. One message was enough."

The senator's free hand trembled slightly. He slipped it in the pocket of his silk dressing gown. "Then what took you so long?"

Davies shrugged. "You know how it is in the spy business.

Globe-trotting, jetting here and there at a moment's notice."

Hastings snorted. "More likely bed-hopping. Never mind; I don't really care, as long as you're here now."

Davies sat up, indignant. "How do you know I haven't been on a top secret mission?"

"Because the Treasury Department wouldn't *give* you a top secret mission. I phoned Bob Anderson at Alcohol, Tobacco, and Firearms. He had no idea where you were."

"Your pal doesn't know everything," Davies sneered.

"He knows everything you *should* have been doing, which is more than you seem to know. Now that he's had to work with the type of person I vouch for—you—I doubt he'll be my pal, as you put it, much longer."

Davies clicked his tongue against the roof of his mouth. "Watch your blood pressure, Uncle. Remember what the doctor said."

"Doctor Stevens doesn't have you for a nephew."

Allen Davies zipped up his suit again, defiantly. The metal clasp grabbed a chest hair. His wincing spoiled the effect.

"You've done wonders for my credibility lately, Allen. I'd love to let you stew in some of the messes you've made."

Davies slowly settled back, draping a leg over the lounger's arm. He ran a hand through his thick, shag-cut hair, and adjusted his headband. "I've often thought you felt that way. But then there are the papers in my mother's safe-deposit box, aren't there? I don't like to bring the subject up, but you ought to keep it in mind, eh? Your mistakes?"

Hastings noticed his glass was empty, though he didn't recall draining it. He reached without thinking for the bottle.

"You're making things increasingly difficult for me, Allen. Gaffes of such magnitude cannot be covered up indefinitely. I've been buying time by shifting you from one organization to another but I'm running out of agencies. In another year I won't be able to get you a job mowing the White House lawn."

Davies leapt to his feet, bouncing on the plush carpet. His nostrils flared. "I don't like your talking to me like that. Neither does Mom."

Bourbon slipped past the senator's lips untasted. "Don't

bring up my sister. You only had to follow instructions. Is it so difficult to listen to the people you work for?"

Davies's lip curled. "Bunch of desk jockeys. What do they know about spying? No imagination."

"Imagination is not the most important quality in espionage work. Getting the job done is what counts. Look at that assignment I got for you at the Office."

"Errand Boy! What a demeaning title *that* was!"

Hastings closed his eyes and sighed. "It's *supposed* to sound trivial. Several highly trained agents would give their right arms for the position. On my say-so, you jumped over them. All you had to do was pick up some microfilm in Manila and bring it back to Washington. The film was already concealed in a bogus silver dollar, but you had to embellish the scheme, didn't you?"

"My plan was sound. I might've been robbed."

"So you thought that forcing a psychic surgeon to implant the coin in your skin was a smart idea."

"Sure. I got it from a book on diamond smugglers. They had normal operations, though. The scars gave them away." Davies sat down again. "It's not my fault that sneaky little Filipino palmed the damned thing!"

Hastings set down his empty glass with a crash, and moved quickly to the other side of the room. An evening with his nephew could empty the liquor cabinet, if he wasn't careful. He perched on an unpadded straight-back chair.

"What about the CIA job? A simple fact-gathering mission in Moscow. Who told you to bribe a leader of the Communist Party to defect?"

"That would have been a political coup!"

"It would have been a political disaster if you hadn't been laughed out of Russia before the Ministry of Propaganda got wind of the story!" The senator's eyes were watery from his outburst. His nose was swollen and purple with broken blood vessels.

Davies shook his head. "If you took your medicine regularly and stopped drinking, you wouldn't have these choleric fits."

"Yes," Hastings hissed. "My medicine."

Davies crossed his arms in front of his chest. "Just why did you want to see me, Uncle? My time is limited, you know."

Not limited enough, the senator thought. "It concerns that FBI stake-out in Cleveland...."

Davies was on his feet again, towering over the older man. "You can't blame that on me! Chavez was on foot; it didn't make sense to follow him in a van. It was just bad luck that he had two accomplices waiting in that alley behind the hospital."

Stay calm, Hastings told himself, biting his lower lip. "Of course it was, Allen. Who could have thought that a man without hands would need help to escape?"

Davies smiled. "That's right, Uncle. There's hope for you yet. Even James Bond can't anticipate everything. In his last movie...."

"For God's sake, Allen, forget the spy films! You only had to shadow Chavez for three blocks!" Hastings slumped in his chair. Dressing gown sleeves hung loose on pipestem arms. He looked ten years older than he was, and felt twenty years older. He could still change his mind, pretend he'd forgotten, that it was some trivial family matter he'd wanted to discuss. Davies would chalk it up to senility.

But the senator's sister wouldn't. Agnes found out about everything sooner or later. She'd never believe Hastings was ignorant of the Chavez information, not in his position. She'd want to know why Allen hadn't been in on the terrorist's recapture.

"Allen," he continued softly, "there's an opportunity for you to make up for that fiasco in Cleveland."

Davies studied his manicured fingernails. "I don't have anything to make up for. If the police had listened to me in the first place...."

"Yes, yes, I know. How would you like to capture the most wanted terrorist in the country?"

Davies narrowed his eyes. "Who?"

Hastings gripped the edge of his seat, knuckles whitening. "Rodicio Chavez."

Davies clasped his hands together with a loud clap and held them above his head. His Adidas did a little dance, rubbing mud and snow deeper into the carpet's pile. "You bet your ass I'd like a second crack at that freak. That would put me in solid with the Bureau, and I could tell your buddy Anderson where he can stick his T-man badge! There's no glamour hiking Kentucky highlands looking for illegal stills, or tracking interstate cigarette smugglers. Double-0 seven wouldn't do it."

"I suppose not." Hastings suddenly noticed he was standing by the liquor cabinet, bourbon bottle in hand, alcohol evaporating coolly on his lips. He shook his head, replaced the bottle, and returned stiff-legged to his uncomfortable chair. "Arthur Blanchard..." he began.

"That lardass from the Office? How is he maligning me now?"

The senator's fingers creaked against the smooth wooden frame of his chair. "I'm betraying a confidence, Allen. Please don't interrupt."

"Okay, Unc. Spill it."

Hastings licked his lips. "Blanchard's daughter was kidnaped a few days ago by a group claiming to be the Free Thought Alliance. Blanchard was involved in the original capture of Rodicio Chavez, and the kidnapping so soon after Chavez's escape is assumed to be more than coincidental. With my influence as a member of the Senate Security Committee, I've so far been able to block further action on the part of the Office, as well as other agencies, such as the FBI, from whom Blanchard could legitimately ask help in rescuing her. I can stall for another twenty hours or so, and I'm afraid that's all the head start I can give you." Hastings grimaced. "You've already lost two days."

"What's a couple of days?" asked Davies, rubbing his hands in glee. "I'll have that turkey nailed to a wall in half an hour. Hot damn! *This* is what spying is all about. A score to settle with an old enemy ... a beautiful damsel in distress ... though if she's Blanchard's kid, I don't suppose she'll be too beautiful. Yes, I shall avenge myself on the arch-fiend Rodicio Chavez. This time, only one of us shall survive!"

"If I could only believe that," Hastings muttered.

"What, Uncle?"

"Isn't death an extreme revenge for a bump on the head?"

"Not for bumps on the heads of Americans everywhere."

"Um. I think the FBI would prefer him alive."

"That's up to the worthless dog. If he'll take his punishment like a man, I'll not deny him a decent gesture." Davies spun on his toes and hurried to the door. Hastings stood.

"Allen!"

"No more time for chit-chat, Unc. I've got work to do!"

"Would you like to know where Chavez is?"

Davies stared down at his own hand on the doorknob for a long moment. Then he grinned sheepishly at his uncle. "Sure. Every little bit of information is useful to an agent."

"I thought it might be," Hastings said softly. "Andrea Blanchard was on assignment in southern Florida when she was kidnapped."

"I'll be damned. She's a spy?"

"No. A reporter."

"Gotcha. I won't blow her cover. She knows how to pick a territory, though. Guess it helps if your father's the boss. Miami Beach! Playground of the jet set! The rich and beautiful! Hey!" he shouted, eyes glittering. "Wouldn't her old man have a fit if she and I got...."

"Not Miami," Hastings interrupted quickly. "The Great Cypress Swamp, just north of Everglades National Park."

Davies frowned. "Not many rich and beautiful there."

"No."

The young man shrugged. "Still, jungles have an air of romance. Alligators and so forth. I remember when Bond was trapped in a pit of...."

"Allen, listen to me," Hastings said, with very little hope that his nephew *would*. He never had before. "This is not a movie. The girl is probably dead by now. The Alliance is made up of ruthless fanatics. If you want to get Chavez, you'll have to do some *real* investigating, and in less than one day."

Davies started nodding halfway through his uncle's speech. "Sure, Unc, I know. I'll catch the first plane in the morning for Miami."

"There's a final night flight in an hour. I think you can still make it."

Davies clapped a hand to his own wrist and pressed a button that lit the face of his watch. He received a digital read-out of time, day, and year. The bright red glow was visible across the room.

"No, can't make it," he decided. "I need time to pack. I don't know where my swim trunks are."

Hastings's eyes rolled to stare at the white ceiling. "How much clothing do you need for one day?"

Davies pursed his lips and glared at his uncle through slits of eyelids. This was one of his most sinister expressions, or so it seemed when he practiced it in a mirror. "You're not trying to tell an experienced field agent how to do his job, are you?"

Hastings closed his eyes and gently rubbed the bridge of his nose. "God forbid. I feel responsible enough as it is."

"Good. People shouldn't try things they aren't qualified to do."

The senator choked back the first words that came to his tongue. Instead, he asked, "You'll tell your mother how I look out for your interests?"

"Sure thing, Unc. She'll be tickled pink. Maybe I can get you an invite to Sunday dinner."

The memory of the odor of scorched pot roast filled Hastings's mind. "Don't go out of your way on my account."

"No problem. What are families for? See you later, Unc."

Hastings listened to his nephew's bouncing tread echo in the hall, and the slam of the outside door. Or perhaps the wind had shut the door, since Allen was never too careful about such things. The senator strayed back to the liquor cabinet and fingered the half-empty bourbon bottle. He held it up to the light, studying the rich wood paneling through its bronze translucence. Shaking his head, the old man replaced the bottle and lurched toward his desk.

Stiff fingers fumbled ineffectually with the handle of the top right drawer. He braced one hand on the desk top and yanked the drawer out with the other. Plastic pill bottles rattled.

Rudolph Hastings scooped up a handful of reserpine tablets, and another handful of apresoline. He gulped them down dry. He reached for the diuretic next, then changed his mind. He wanted the oblivion of sleep now, if he could manage it at all, and he couldn't if he had to spend half the night in the bathroom.

He contemplated emptying the contents of the drawer into the toilet. Let his blood pressure take its toll. A fatal stroke would solve the problem of Allen Davies as far as he was concerned.

No. Agnes would think he'd done it on purpose, to frustrate her boy's ambitions. Why give her the satisfaction of being right once more?

THIRTEEN

Two figures made their way through the swamp, the wet ground sucking at their boot heels. Mosquitos swarmed, disturbed, but Tom had become inured to their bites, and the insects avoided Blood altogether. Like the vampire, they desired living food. They had no use for carrion.

Tom halted abruptly. Blood reached from behind to grasp the youth's shoulder. He'd tried to bolt several times already.

Tom's head swiveled from side to side, searching. Searching for something he did not want to find.

"How much further?" Blood demanded. The forceful command in the agent's voice was all that had kept Tom stable. Apparently that would not be enough when they reached the scene of tragedy.

"There! Through that grove, and…."

The shoulder quavered under Blood's icy grip. "Steady," the vampire ordered.

"The thing!" Tom screeched. "It's come back! It's come for me!" With a surge of energy, Tom tore loose. He charged blindly into a thick patch of foliage.

Blood threw down the khaki scrap that remained in his hand, swore silently, and plunged in after Tom. Razor-sharp edges of the high sawgrass slashed his hands and face, but he did not bleed. The cuts healed quickly.

Tom stumbled over every log and root in his path. He did not stop even when he fell, but crawled forward until he regained his footing.

Blood's night vision allowed him to circumvent these obstacles, but in so doing he could not make full use of the speed latent in his powerful leg muscles. The vampire begrudged the few seconds this cost him, although he would obviously soon catch up to Tom. He really wanted to examine the clearing where, according to Tom, some kind of skirmish had taken place, and it was getting late. If he were still here at dawn, when he'd be trapped in human form to avoid perishing in sunlight, running water could keep him prisoned until the tides lowered again around noon.

Blood was tempted to let Tom go, but he hadn't quite squeezed him dry of information. Or anything else.

Tom was almost in arm's reach when he suddenly dropped from sight. The vampire stopped dead, defying inertia. As his feral eyes drank in the shadowy details ahead, his keen ears picked up a faint sound: the echo of a splash that had originally been lost in the crashing din of the chase.

Blood eased his right foot forward. The ground beneath his boot sole turned to jelly.

Tom had plunged headfirst into a patch of bog. Only his long legs, from knee to toe, were visible, and they were being greedily sucked down.

Blood knelt. One hand felt for the edge of the pit. Rooting himself firmly on the lip of solid ground, he reached forward with his right arm. Long, powerful fingers clutched the heel and ankle of Tom's boot. Blood pulled.

The footwear fell apart in his hand. Tom continued to sink, now just out of reach.

Tom was doomed. Unless ....

Shape-shifting to traditional vampiric forms was fairly simple, and Blood had discovered that with an extra dab of will power he could become a master of disguise and survive such exotic environments as the floor of the South China Sea. But that had been cosmetic adaptation, with known forms to refer to. This would be something new, a modification of a familiar shape. The idea was as mad as the glint in Tom's eyes had been.

Dropping the remnants of boot, Blood reached forth again for Tom's now bare foot. It had sunk almost to the ankle. There was a gap of almost a meter from his fingers. Blood strained forward stretching out for the foot .... stretching ... stretching ....

His right arm grew to half again its normal length. It had worked!

Long, pale fingers plunged beneath the surface of the slough and wrapped around the leg just above the ankle. The body sank no further.

Slowly, because of the poor leverage, Blood raised the leg out of the mire. When he was able at last to get a two-handed grip, he dragged Tom free completely, and lay him on his back on solid ground.

Blood cleared muck from Tom's mouth and nostrils, but the youth was not breathing. The agent bent over the slime-covered form and pushed down hard on sternum.

Nothing.

He pushed again. Again. Again.

Tom sputtered suddenly, coughing up black, oily water. His stomach quivered. Blood continued pressing, forcing up more slime. At least he would not have to try mouth-to-mouth resuscitation. He doubted his death's breath could instill life.

Tom's eyes opened at last, but they were marred by an opaque glaze. Soft, whispered gibberish spewed from filth-dribbling lips; unrelated phonemes of no possible meaning. Blood grimaced. Tom's mind was gone. Only the body remained, of use to the agent for only one purpose.

Fastidiously, Blood wiped slick mud from Tom's throat. His fingers trembled as they felt the pulse of hot, flowing blood. His eyes shone red with the thirst. Lips drew back from needle-sharp canines. The agent bent nearer the half drowned youth.

Blood fed.

Tom's opaque eyes slowly lost their sheen. His lips fluttered, mouthing a few final unintelligible phrases, and then fell still.

Blood's chin was stained with crimson when he finally pulled away from the corpse. Perhaps a liter remained in those collapsing veins, but he'd had enough for now. The thirst, the lust, had been slaked. There was other work to do, such as disposing of Tom properly.

In a secret pocket of Blood's jacket were what looked like half a dozen cold capsules. In fact, each contained a special decay-speeding bacteria culture that was activated by exposure to air ... and food. The bacteria attacked any organic substance within reach, and when that was done the micro-organisms devoured themselves. Only Blood was permitted this highly dangerous method of corpse-disposal. Only Blood needed to so thoroughly destroy those he slew ... or risk an epidemic as his victims turned to vampires themselves.

The capsules remained in their secret pocket. There was no way to isolate Tom's body from the wealth of surrounding organic matter. If a single bacterium escaped in this life-teeming swamp it would grow and reproduce uncontrollably. The Everglades, the Florida peninsula, the continent... in weeks, the entire world might be denuded of life.

Blood had two other options: burn the body, or dismember it. The first might advertise his presence, which would interfere with his examination of the clearing.

Distaste mingled with an animalistic satisfaction he could not wholly deny, as Blood rended Tom's corpse with teeth and nails and brute strength. One by one, Blood tossed the dead man's limbs into the bog from which the agent had dragged him minutes earlier.

Blood paused suddenly, in the middle of his grisly task. He sensed alien eyes upon him. He looked up. There, almost invisible in the shadowy vegetation, a massive lumbering form seemed to move away from him. A tough tendon distracted Blood for an instant. When he looked again, the shape was gone.

A scavenger, smelling death, seeking a free meal?

At last, Tom's headless torso was consigned to its oozing grave. Blood washed off the gore in a shallow pool, and entered the clearing Tom had dreaded.

Death had surely visited here. The swamp had reclaimed most traces of human invasion, but Blood found marks to indicate that two to four bodies had been dragged from here. Some rope fibers hung from an upcurved mangrove root.

Blood found a rifle underneath a fallen log. The weapon's stock was shattered, and its barrel clogged with mud. Anyone trying to fire this would be committing suicide. This was the gun Tom had tried to retrieve when he was frightened off by ... something.

The skunk-ape?

Perhaps that angle was not as futile as Blood had thought. Ranger Hernandez had certainly seen *something* she didn't recognize, something she felt worth reporting, and she grew up in this wilderness.

Meanwhile, Sheriff Paul Rudge could trace this gun. It looked like an ordinary hunting rifle, fairly new despite its battered condition. There should be serial numbers, or remnants of same. The buyer had probably used a false name, but aliases often contained subtle clues to a person's identity or habits, if one knows how to read them. Most of the names Blood used did.

The wind was hardly strong enough to qualify as a breeze, but Blood detected its shift. The tide was returning. He'd have to hurry back now. He'd hoped for a look at Holroyd Hummock, which if he was not mistaken lay not far from here. But that was just a hunch, and what he'd gotten from Tom was likely far more valuable.

And, of course, he'd saved some time by not having to hunt.

FOURTEEN

Edward Kovacs halted beside a Sour Orange rootstock tree that had succumbed to exocortis virus right before the winter's first big freeze. He shifted his shotgun to ease the cramp in his right arm, and leaned against the shattered trunk. From this angle, he could just make out a light in the window of the box frame house he shared with his partner and fellow bachelor, Chester Sciati. Patrolling their orange grove was proving more exhausting than either man anticipated, considering how small it was.

Kovacs rubbed his ungloved hands together, then stuck them under his armpits. The fingers weren't so much cold as stiff. He'd be glad when winter was over. It was a stark time of year, even in south Florida. Three hours of sleep snatched in ten and fifteen minute clumps during the day was nowhere near enough. He was getting a headache from the night air on his scalp, even with his knit cap pulled down to the ears. And his feet itched from the sandy soil that seeped into his loose-fitting boots and somehow even worked its way under the thick socks. He rubbed his right instep on a protruding root of the dead tree. The foot still itched.

A scuffling sound came from behind. Kovacs didn't bother turning. He knew Chester's tread too well to mistake it for another's.

Chester Sciati had lean, sharp features and a thick mat of platinum hair. He'd been a guard in the Minneapolis department store where Kovacs worked as a window dresser. Both men had tired of the bitter midwestern winters at the same time, three years earlier, and they'd pooled their savings to purchase this grove. Through loans and luck they'd kept the grove operating, and their struggle was on the verge of paying off. Their marketing co-op was merging with two others, and with improved distribution and a better bargaining position the K&S Grove might even show a profit next year. Consequently, they were more than usually jealous of every orange. When other local growers reported a rash of pilferage in the area, Sciati suggested a night watch, and Kovacs readily agreed.

"Seen anything, Ed?"

Kovacs shook his head. "Looks like I've lost another night's beauty sleep for nothing, Chet."

"Not for nothing. Protecting our investment."

"From what? We've patrolled every night this week, and who have we caught? Three skinny ten-year-olds who couldn't carry off a dozen oranges combined."

"Which means that our night watch is already effective, as a deterrent," Sciati countered. "Just because we haven't been hit yet doesn't mean we won't be. Grayson and Petrovich have each lost two whole trees' worth since Sunday." Kovacs grunted. "So they say."

Moonlight played along Sciati's silvery hair as he turned to his partner with a sharp, narrow look. "What are you suggesting, Ed?"

"Walking around in the dark gives a man time to think, Chet. Suppose the other growers want our grove? Mightn't they try to scare us off with stories?" Sciati laughed. "I'm the one who suspects everyone, Chet, remember? You never had to outsmart a shoplifter. Ours is the least productive grove in the co-op. Probably in the whole state. We'd have to pay someone to take it off our hands." Kovacs shrugged. "It was just an idea. I didn't say it was a good one. Here's another: the others are pulling our legs. After three years, these crackers still call us damned Yankees."

"It's not half as clever as the stories they told us when we first came down." Kovacs sighed. "Maybe I'm getting paranoid in my dotage."

"You're just punchy from lack of sleep. Give me the shotgun and go to bed. I'll wake you for breakfast."

The weapon's barrel was cold to the balding man's touch as he handed it over. "That must be it. I can't take many more long nights, Chet. Neither can you. We'll have to hire help."

"I've been thinking the same thing. The trick is finding someone reliable."

"How about that fellow who showed us those good fishing spots? If he's not interested, he'll surely know someone."

"Frank Jordan? Didn't I tell you? He was lost in the swamp a few days back. They found his boat."

Kovacs frowned. "If you did, it didn't register. Jeez, that's a shame. He was the first one down here ... Chet?"

"What?"

"Over there. By that Rough Lemon stock."

Sciati turned slowly, because he didn't want to alarm the trespasser. His body tensed. He stared at the stock tree for a long moment. Then he raised the shotgun, bracing its stock against his shoulder.

"What the *hell* is that?" he whispered.

Something huge and dark moved against the night. In the shadowy grove, it resembled at first a stolid cypress that had wandered out of the surrounding marsh, having forgotten that it couldn't walk.

Sciati crouched low and stole forward quietly. Kovacs followed suit. The shape became more humanoid as they drew near, but there was still something unhuman about it. The head was hidden in the tree's lower branches. Moonlight glinted off a wire basket that dangled from a hand the size of a man's skull. The other hand was busy among the branches, lowering from time to time clutching the pick of K&S Grove's meager crop.

"Whatever it is," Kovacs replied,

"It's stripping one of our best trees." Sciati took another cautious step. "I wonder ... it looks like that skunk-ape Yablonski was raving about at the last co-op meeting."

"It's sure not any local critter."

"Maybe it's a gorilla that escaped from the circus wintering grounds."

"Are you going to shoot it or classify it?"

"Ssh. We're in hearing range now."

Both men could hear the metallic chunk-chunk as orange after orange bounced into the wire basket. The creature took deep, harsh breaths, as if breathing through a wet blanket. Lesser branches cracked sharply as they were shoved aside.

The trespasser's hearing was no less keen. The massive head lowered until two great, watery eyes glared in the direction of the men's voices. The wire basket was set gently on the ground. A warning growl swelled. The creature stepped forward.

Sciati decided he was close enough to shoot.

The blast from the first barrel pebbled the tree trunk, but the second tore a crimson hole in the trespasser's thick arm. The creature hadn't expected that! It staggered back, kicking over the wire basket. Ripe oranges spilled along the sandy soil.

The creature staggered, but did not fall.

"That blast would have knocked over an elephant!" Kovacs exclaimed. "*What* the hell is that?"

A rumbling bass roar threatened to split the sky. Then the creature lunged.

"Let's not find out," Sciati suggested. Without pausing to reload, he sprinted toward the house.

Kovacs was right behind him, though he fell behind a few meters. Thirty months of subsistence orange growing had helped toughen Kovacs's portly frame, but Sciati had the superior stamina of a man who worked to stay in top condition.

Sciati was on the porch and through the back door before his partner reached the lowest step.

In his haste, Kovacs tripped over that step, sprawling forward. His arms shot up just in time to protect his skull; the elbow hit the porch edge, sending a jolt of pain down to his fingertips.

The creature roared again. The wooden steps seemed to vibrate.

Gasping for air, Kovacs half crawled, half pulled himself onto the porch. Splinters ripped his palms, yet the rough wood seemed slick as ice when he tried to gain his footing. He could feel the monster reaching for his neck, its fetid breath searing his fringe of hair.

The back door slammed open then, and Sciati was silhouetted in the doorway, shotgun ready. He'd taken time to reload.

"Keep your head down, Ed."

Kovacs gasped assent, and turned to glance behind. The creature was not as near as he'd thought. Despite its inhuman stride, the friable soil had slowed it even more than the men, due to its greater weight. It was five meters from the porch steps, though closing quickly, when Jerry let both barrels fly.

Metal fragments patterned the creature's chest. Something wet spattered on Kovacs's pate. The creature slowed.

It did not stop.

"What the hell *is* that?" Sciati muttered as he helped Kovacs into the house.

"That thing can't be real. I must have walking malaria." Every word Kovacs spoke was punctuated by a gulp for air. His heart seemed ready to burst, and his shirt was soaked with sweat.

Sciati slammed and bolted the door. "I wish to Christ you did, Ed. I wish we both had swamp fever: If that thing decides to come in, I don't think we can do anything about it."

Kovacs stood shaking a moment, bracing himself against a table. Then he staggered to the gun cabinet. Aside from the shotgun, their only weapons were two rarely-used hunting rifles. These packed more power than the double-barreled weapon, but required greater skill for a hit. At close range, though, the rifles might be enough to kill the creature, if he or Sciati could hit a vital area.

Assuming the creature *had* any vital areas.

A rifle and a box of ammunition apiece were distributed. Then Sciati turned off the light.

The porch door held, because no attempt was made to breach it. The grove reverberated with groanings and crashings, but at a distance from the house. The creature was venting its rage elsewhere ... or building up to a final assault. Sciati crawled to the window and raised his head just enough to peer out.

He could see nothing but shadows, any one of which seemed to move if he stared at it long enough.

In time, the sounds came to an abrupt halt.

Kovacs and Sciati spent the rest of the night crouched behind their sparse furniture. Fingers cramped on trigger guards.

As the night sky began to lighten, Kovacs licked his lips,

noticing for the first time that the bottom one had split. "I guess we scared it off," he said, crossing his fingers.

Sciati did not reply. He slowly rose to his feet and walked to the door. The scrape of his boots on the hardwood floor was the only sound he made, until he unbolted the door. Metal squealed on metal in the silence. He took a deep breath, cradled the rifle in his right arm, and yanked the door wide open.

He swallowed a dry lump in his throat.

A score of orange trees had been uprooted, and were stacked before the porch like an enormous, untidy pile of firewood, blocking the steps completely. Oranges littered the ground as far as the white-haired man could see, filling the holes where the trees had stood.

Kovacs joined his partner on stiffened legs. Together, they gazed numbly over the chaos.

"That's it, then," Kovacs said at last, his voice cracking. "I wonder if the store will take us back."

Sciati's lips thinned to an almost invisible line. His eyes glittered hot cobalt. "I won't go back to Minnesota."

Kovacs's eyes were moist. "What else can we do?"

Sciati unloaded the rifle. "See if the truck is all right. I'll fix breakfast."

"A last meal and a drive into the Gulf of Mexico?"

Sciati smiled weakly at the concern in his partner's voice. "No, Ed. The sheriff's office is far enough."

"Of course. We'll have to report this to Paul Rudge. What can he do, though, Chet? Arrest that thing? Handcuffs don't come that large."

Sciati's smile strengthened. "Rudge knows the mechanics of applying for Federal Disaster Relief. He's filled out forms for hundreds of hurricane victims."

Kovacs widened his eyes. "I forgot about aid programs. The co-op office has forms, too, and they're closer."

Sciati shook his head. "Arlo couldn't begin to explain how we should file in a situation like this. Rudge may doubt our story, and he may think we've been hitting the local brew too hard, but he'll tell us how we can present the case without sounding like a couple of lunatics, and back us up besides."

FIFTEEN

Dawn tinted the crowns of surrounding cypress. Blood's mud-caked boots scraped the macadam of the Tamiami Trail. His canines retreated until they were no longer than normal teeth, and his ear tips grew more rounded, before the sun's first rays could touch him.

Brown and black streaked the agent's safari jacket, along with a few dark red flecks at the collar. He carried the barrel and shattered stock of a hunting rifle in one hand. He considered changing to fresh clothes, and decided not to waste the time. He wasn't planning to keep his nocturnal excursion a secret, only certain details, and vanity was for the living.

Instead, Blood headed for the careless-looking shack that Paul Rudge used for a sheriff's office. Rudge wouldn't be in this early, but Blood could review the files, bearing in mind that at least some of the complainants really *had* seen something.

The building faced northwest, and its front was in shadow. Blood was halfway up the dusty driveway when he noticed that the door stood wide open.

The agent paused. He'd anticipated no difficulty with the lock, but this was too easy. People in rural Florida might be more casual about locking up than those in inner-city Washington, but surely that wouldn't apply to a sheriff's office.

Blood moved to the side of the path, into waist-high sawgrass. His human form was vulnerable, and he did not wish to waste an entire day as a corpse. Not now, when things were starting to happen. If Blood was not the catalyst, at least he'd fallen into the mixture at the right moment.

He crept forward, ready to hurl himself into thick sedge at

the first glint of a gun barrel, the first click of a bullet falling into its chamber.

The gray wooden steps of the veranda were reached without incident.

The boards bore dark brown stains. Bootprints. Blood did not have to examine them closely. He knew the faint, copper scent well.

He avoided the steps and leapt over the chest-high railing. His feet struck the planking as silently as a cat's. The creak of the boards was no louder than a mouse's squeal. Blood flattened against the wall beside the open door.

Concentrating, Blood filtered out the sounds of the waking swampland. His ears could detect no movement inside the structure. There was, however, respiration, faint and quavering. One breather. One was all you needed for a trap.

Yet the gasping rang of agony, not anticipation.

Blood entered, moving quickly to minimize himself as a target. The outer reception room was empty. He rushed past the desk belonging to Rudge's deputy, who'd been out on patrol when Blood had been here earlier. The door to Rudge's office was ajar and Blood hit it running, slamming it open. Framed citations rattled on the wall.

That his caution had been superfluous did not embarrass the agent. Dignity at the wrong moment could be fatal.

A naked Paul Rudge was spread-eagled across his scarred oak desk. Barbed wire coiled around his wrists and ankles, and stretched down to entangle each of the four sturdy desk legs. The sheriff's body, slight but well-toned, was crisscrossed with bright red welts. Strips of flesh hung raw from the edges of these wounds. Caked blood coated the man's lips, and crimson liquid still oozed from razor slashes in his cheeks. The right eye was closed by swollen flesh, but the left fluttered at the sound of Blood's entrance.

Rudge's lips moved soundlessly, finally rasping out "Who?" before the voice broke in a dry cough. Cracked lips bled afresh.

Blood was subject to intense and often overwhelming bloodlust, but Rudge's lettings did not tempt him. Outrage forestalled the burning hunger. Men dared to call *his* kind inhuman!

He put down the shattered gun.

Rudge's lips quivered again.

"Don't talk," Blood ordered. "It's Cuardi. The reporter. You'll be all right now."

The sheriff's mouth relaxed.

In a screened alcove, Blood found a brown-stained enamel sink. On a shelf beside it stood a ceramic pitcher with a chunk missing from the lip. Blood shook the pitcher upside down to evict any insects, while he let rusty tap water run until the pipes cleared. Then he filled the pitcher to the gap in its brim and carried it slowly to the man on the desk.

Rudge opened his good eye as the thin, dark-haired agent came into view. "They ... they...."

"In a minute." There was a soothing tone in Blood's voice that he had not used in decades, thought himself incapable of using again. "Drink some water first."

The agent dipped long, thin fingers into the pitcher, and moistened Rudge's lips. The sheriff's swollen tongue lapped it up. He seemed oblivious to the cold touch of Blood's dead flesh. After a few more wettings to clean the caked blood from the man's mouth, the vampire brought the pitcher closer. The old man struggled to raise his head. Blood helped support him with his free hand.

Rudge sipped very little before his head sank back. Blood lowered it gently. The sheriff took a deep breath, and his face twisted in agony.

Blood lightly ran an icy hand along Rudge's torso. He frowned. At least two ribs were broken, and one might have punctured a lung.

"Wire-cutters," Rudge rasped. "Top left drawer."

Blood opened the drawer slowly, to avoid jarring the desk. He snipped the bonds as close to the wrists and ankles as possible. The wire was thick with rust and filth, and the barbs bit deep. The wounds needed thorough cleaning. Rudge would have to endure tetanus shots, if he lived long enough to receive them.

Rudge wriggled his fingers, trying to reach the pitcher Blood had left beside his right hip. He didn't have the strength to move the hand itself. Blood stilled his motions with a touch. A stack of police equipment catalogs pillowed Rudge's head, and the pitcher was moved up so the man could sip simply by turning his neck.

Then Blood unwound the barbed wire manacles.

Rudge inhaled sharply as the first barb ripped free, but made no complaint. The soles of his feet itched, and for distraction the sheriff tried to rub them together. Only the right leg responded.

Blood paused and looked at Rudge's battered face with a raised eyebrow. "I think it's broken," said Rudge.

Blood glanced at the ugly rainbow of black, blue and green swelling below Rudge's left knee. "I think so, too. We'll get to it."

Rudge nodded, wincing.

"You shouldn't talk more than necessary," the agent continued, "but there are things I must know, and talking will take your mind off what I'm doing. Who did this?"

"Five men. Yankees. Twenties, early thirties. Strangers."

"What did they want?"

"Answers. Asked about some friends supposedly arrested for illegal camping in the 'glades. I didn't know about them, and said so." Rudge smiled weakly. "Guess they didn't believe me."

"Did they ask about anything else?"

"That gal reporter...."

"Andrea Blanchard? There, that's one wrist done."

"Yep. I'm afraid I told them everything I told you, which was everything I knew. Only thing I could add...."

The sentence was stifled by another sharp intake of breath as Blood pulled wire out of particularly deep gouges. The wounds trickled fresh blood as the agent worked the pointed edges loose, but he had no alternative. Rudge's hands were cold. The wires blocked his circulation. They could not be left in place. "The ankles won't be as bad," Blood promised.

Rudge swallowed hard, and took a long sip of water before going on. "I told them about you, working on her story. Guess I shouldn't have."

"You had little choice."

"They'll probably go after you next."

"I'd like that," said Blood, with a grim smile, "but why should they? They're not interested in skunk-apes."

"No more than you, eh?"

Blood did not reply. He moved down to the ankles. Despite his assurances, the wire here was drawn even tighter. Getting the wire-cutter around the metal strands without scraping already raw flesh was difficult and time-consuming. Blood could have snapped the wire in his bare hands in seconds, but the pressure would have increased the pain unbearably for Rudge.

"I pegged you for a private dick yesterday," the sheriff went on, "Figured it wasn't my business, though. If it became my business, you'd know where to come."

"You'd better rest. Don't tire yourself talking."

"Hell, son, talk never killed a man. I'm grateful my tongue still works." The last loop of wire came loose in Blood's hand. Its barbs burrowed into his palm. He tossed it in a corner.

"This doesn't make sense," Blood muttered. "What you told them, you would have freely told anyone. They didn't have to torture you."

"They didn't. Not until after."

The agent's eyes flared. "Why?"

"Pure orneriness, I reckon. The leader, a fat kid dressed in white, made a nasty remark. Can't remember what, now. I got nasty right back, and a little careless. One of them cracked my skull from behind. Next thing I knew I was Paul Rudge, human pin-cushion."

Blood found Rudge's first aid kit on the same shelf the pitcher had been on. He snapped it open. A yellowed scrap of paper had been taped to the inside of the lid, but the tape was old. The scrap drifted to the floor. Blood retrieved it, and glanced at outmoded emergency procedures for snakebite.

Paul Rudge had been bitten by a snake called the Free Thought Alliance, and he was only their most recent victim.

Blood placed a bottle of antiseptic and a roll of cotton on top of the desk. "This will sting," he warned. He soaked the cotton and rubbed it gently into the punctures.

Rudge hissed at the first touch, but flinched no further. "Son," he said, "right now you could let an alligator breakfast on my right leg, and a cougar gnaw on my left, and I'd think I'd been bit by a mosquito."

"You'll feel it more when the shock wears off. Who should I call for an ambulance?"

"From here? No one. They pulled the phones out of the wall."

Blood glanced at the floor. Forms, file folders, and personal trinkets littered the office where the FTA had thrown them in their haste to clear the desktop. The telephone lay on its side, the receiver alongside, the cord coiled around it. The ragged end mocked Blood with a score of copper tongues.

"I passed a gas station. I'll call from there."

"Center drawer has a list of numbers. Call my deputy, too. Charlie Grimm. Somebody's got to clean this place up."

Blood slid open the center drawer as gently as he had the other. He folded the list into his reporter's notebook, leaving both drawers open.

He picked up the rifle he'd dropped. "I found this gun in the swamp. It might belong to one of the men who did this. Can Charlie trace it?"

Rudge forced a smile. "I'd hate to try stopping him."

Blood laid the gun across the open drawers.

"I don't know how long the ambulance will take. If I leave, will you be all right?"

"I can't get much worse. My back's stiffening up. I wish you could get me to the cot on the corner, but I'd best stay put. No telling what's busted inside."

Blood found Rudge's torn uniform blouse in the rubble and laid it over the man's midriff and crotch.

"Cuardi." Rudge's voice was fading. Blood leaned forward to catch his words.

"Yes, Sheriff?"

"Those bastards thought I was dead meat. I heard them talk before they left. The fat kid said they were going to the Holroyd ruins. Tell Charlie that."

"I will." Blood started to move away.

Rudge forced his hand to move, latching on to the vampire's wrist.

"Tell him they have guns, too. Military weapons. He ought to call the governor. This looks big."

"I promise I'll tell him, Sheriff. Relax." Blood eased himself from the man's weak grip, and stared into his swollen, bleary eye. "Rest," he continued. "Sleep. Feel no pain."

Under the spell of those deep, soft, brown eyes, Rudge's eyelid fell. The agent's voice became a murmur, then tapered to nothing. The man's chest rose and fell smoothly and regularly, now that Blood's suggestion blocked his sensations of pain. Rudge would sleep peacefully until an ambulance arrived with medical attendants and chemical pain-killers.

The agent's eyes filled with a horrible red flame as he straightened. There was little more he could do here ... but much he intended to do elsewhere.

Blood's superhuman pace raised man-sized clouds of dust behind him. He slowed, slightly, when he reached Route 41, where he was likely to encounter traffic. A battered pick-up truck approached as he turned onto the main road. He considered hitching a ride to the gas station, but decided against it. The little time saved would be more than offset by the annoyance of questions he was in no mood to respond to. One of the farmers in the cab waved. He ignored them, hurrying on.

SIXTEEN

The white-haired man lowered his hand back inside the cab of the pick-up. "Look at that son of a bitch run, Ed," he said to the driver. "Who the hell does he think he is?"

The other man wore a sour grimace. His stomach churned, trying to digest a pair of undercooked eggs after a sleepless night. His partner could handle a crisis, but he was a lousy cook. Fortunately, they'd been able to salvage a few oranges to eat on the way, though the juice made the steering wheel sticky.

Suddenly the driver's eyes glittered, and his grimace curled into a mischievous grin.

"Why, Chet," he said, "he must've been one of those damned Yankees we keep hearing about."

The cab filled with laughter as the truck turned off the highway onto the driveway leading to the sheriff's office.

SEVENTEEN

"Hernandez!"

Blood's bellow echoed in the ranger station, rattling the loosely mortared windows. The door rebounded from the force of his entrance, slamming shut behind him. A young man with reddish blond hair and a close-trimmed mustache slapped wildly at the reports and survey maps scattering across his desk swept by the sudden rush of wind. The agent ignored him, striding purposefully to the chest-high partition at the rear of the room.

Hernandez stood glaring over the wooden barrier. Her eyes were dark and depthless as she struggled to hold her outrage down to mere contempt. Perhaps she'd decided the Ice Maiden act was the best way to handle a persistent reporter ... if she could keep it up. Or she might be trying to control her temper to impress the high-cheeked young man with thick, curly hair who was sitting in her visitor's chair. Blood doubted that. The ranger was not the type to modify her behavior for a third party.

"We're leaving," Blood ordered. "Now."

Hernandez glanced past Blood's pallid face to her assistant, who was hastily straightening his desk again. "Remind me to thank our sheriff, Bill. Here's *two* people he's recommended my services as a guide to—and both of them fascinated by the Holroyd place. Isn't that a coincidence?"

Curlyhead swiveled at the mention of Holroyd. He peered at Blood through pig-like eyes, and his thick lips curled down.

"Fuck off," he advised.

Hernandez laughed. "I see you two have good manners in common, as well. Al Cuardi, meet Peter Collins—definitely no relation to the founder of Collins county. Or do you already know each other?" Her voice grew hard. "I suppose, Mr. Cuardi, that you got tired waiting for your flunky to draw me out. Well, you've overplayed your hand. I do have plans to visit Holroyd Hummock today, but after this clumsy play I wouldn't lead you two across the street!"

Blood gripped the partition, gouging holes in the soft wood. "I've never seen your friend in olive drab before."

"Of course not! You've no idea who he is!"

"I didn't say that. I have a very good idea. You, Pete, you claim Sheriff Rudge told you to talk to this ranger?"

Collins scowled. "What's it to you?"

"When did you speak to him?"

"None of your fucking business."

"Cut the comedy, Cuardi," Hernandez growled. "You know goddamn well he's never even seen Rudge. You fed him that story to get me to...."

"No." Though flat and controlled, Blood's voice rang imperiously in the cluttered room. "What did *he* tell you?"

A wise-crack poised on the woman's lips. She let it pass. "Collins said he spoke to the sheriff this morning. I called to verify, but the line was dead."

"So was Rudge," Blood said, noting the flicker of a smile on Collins's lips. "Almost. By now he should be in a hospital in Naples."

"Good god." Hernandez sank back in her chair, ignoring her surly, fidgeting visitor. "What happened? An accident?"

"I think not." Blood smiled unpleasantly. "Pete knows more than I. How did you get those stains on your sleeve, Pete?" Blood reached over the partition, pointing a long, thin finger.

Collins jumped from the chair, sending it crashing backward. From a bulging pocket of his jacket he drew a .38 caliber Llama Model VIII automatic pistol. The vampire knew from experience, and the ranger guessed from its appearance, that the weapon was not designed for sport.

"You had your chance to come quietly, bitch,"

Collins snarled. Hernandez could not suppress a chuckle. "You almost had me for a minute, Cuardi, but the B-movie dialogue was too much. You ought to be ashamed, using a sweet old man like Paul to work on my sympathy. Get lost, both of you. I have work to do."

A .38 bullet ripped into her desk. Hernandez leapt to her feet.

"That's better," Collins said. "Now. You, Cuardi, back off. The cunt and I are leaving. And you, Bill, I want you in front of that desk, where I can see your hands."

Bill Arneson clenched his fists in frustration. He could see his revolver resting in the top right drawer. He'd started to reach for it the minute Collins fired. It wasn't loaded, but the punk didn't know that, and the distraction would give Lucy a chance to grab her own automatic. It wouldn't work now, though.

Or would it? Cuardi was backing toward Arneson. In a couple of steps the reporter would block Collins's line of sight.

Arneson went for it.

Blood heard the click of the terrorist's gun, saw it was pointed past his shoulder. The agent was too far from Collins to spoil his aim, even without the partition in his way. Instead, Blood spun around as the explosion sounded, and crashed into the junior ranger. Arneson sprawled backwards across his desk, smashing his knee on its edge. His rearranged papers scattered on the hardwood floor, and Arneson followed.

The bullet gouged a chunk of flesh from Blood's shoulder. The vampire dropped and rolled back against the partition, which afforded his best cover. The wound was deep and, if he permitted it, painful, but he'd only lost some skin and muscle. He wasn't incapacitated ... unless Collins took better aim next time.

A third shot thundered in the ranger station. It had a more subdued quality, with sharper definition. A different gun.

Collins yelped as he staggered back against the wall and sank to his knees. His left hand clutched his abdomen. Crimson welled between the fingers. He stared in shock at Hernandez, and the automatic that had seemed to appear in her hand from nowhere.

Then his eyes flared hatred and he turned his gun on her.

Blood was on him before another shot could be fired. His

long fingers clamped about the terrorist's wrist and squeezed. The Llama clattered to the floor from nerveless fingers. Collins screamed as his wrist bones cracked. A jagged white shard tore through his flesh.

Still the vampire tightened his grip.

"My god, Cuardi!" exclaimed Hernandez, horrified by the cruelty contracting Blood's features. "That's enough! He's harmless now!"

Blood glared up at her resentfully. For a second, it seemed he might attack her as well. Then the savagery drained from his face. He let the limp hand fall, and Collins moaned as it struck the floor.

Blood retrieved the Llama, emptied it, and placed it on the desk near the bullet hole. For a long moment he stared at his own hand, as if more fascinated by the blood that had splashed on it from the terrorist's maimed wrist than the trickle that oozed from his shoulder. Then he met the ranger's wide-eyed gaze.

"You weren't too gentle with him, yourself," he countered. "You could have gone for a limb."

"There wasn't time to pick and choose. A gut wound hurts like hell, but with prompt treatment it's not usually fatal."

She glanced over the partition and saw Bill Arneson using the edge of his desk to haul himself erect. "Bill? Are you all right?"

Arneson stamped his right leg and rubbed the back of his thigh. He winced. There was going to be a beauty of a bruise there by noon.

"Nothing a good rub-down and a healthy dose of common sense won't cure, Lucy. I think I owe you my life, Mr. Cuardi."

Blood nodded absently.

Hernandez nudged the gun on her desk with the muzzle of her own weapon. She turned to Collins, who was curled up in a groaning ball around a widening circle of red. "Did you use this gun on Paul Rudge?" she demanded.

Collins shook his head, then told her what she could do with the Llama.

"Given time," Blood interrupted, "I'd have him begging to talk. But we don't need his answers. Rudge was beaten, tortured and left for dead by Pete and his pals. No doubt a similar fate was planned for you, with a few refinements in honor of your sex."

Hernandez stood over Collins and shifted the grip on her gun as if to strike its butt against the terrorist's skull. She noticed Blood regarding her with grim amusement. Biting her lip, the ranger backed up a pace.

"What kind of people *are* you?"

Rhetoric came easily to Collins, even through his pain. "The wave of the future," he spat. "Destroyers of your obscene, materialistic culture." A coughing spasm speckled his lips with blood.

"Just your average monomaniac," the vampire explained. "The woods are full of them. Especially around Holroyd, if we hurry."

Arneson entered the partitioned cubicle, a towel draped over his shoulder and a first aid kit in hand. For Blood, the space was getting uncomfortably crowded. The graveyard malodor that clung to him was for the moment overwhelmed by the sharp tang of cordite in the air, but that would not last. Even now, Arneson wrinkled his nose as he approached the vampire.

"Can the jacket and shirt be removed?" Arneson asked. "Or should I cut it away?"

The agent glanced at his shoulder. The bleeding had already stopped. "I'm all right. You'd better see to Collins, if you think he's worth the effort." Arneson knelt by the terrorist as Blood stepped from the cubicle.

"Why would they want me?" Hernandez asked.

"Presumably because you know too much about Andrea Blanchard. They've kidnapped her, you know."

Hernandez felt her automatic growing heavy. "Andrea was kidnapped?"

Blood turned to face the ranger over the partition. "You must have suspected something. Andrea Blanchard's been missing for a week. What did you think had happened to her?"

"Nothing, of course!" Hernandez snapped back. "I received no missing persons report. I lent her a radio set so she could call in if there was any trouble." The ranger's lips thinned. "I

know your type, Cuardi. You think women are helpless, brain-
less creatures who need men around to save their asses." When
Blood did not rise to the bait, she added, "Andrea had a solid
basic knowledge of woodlore. I told her where I'd seen the thing,
how to deal with local fauna, what vegetation was safe to eat ...
everything I knew about the hummock."

"What you knew obviously wasn't enough." Blood's eyes
narrowed. "So you admit you saw something?"

Hernandez hissed. Damn her temper! She hadn't meant to
reveal so much. She nodded.

"I couldn't even guess what it was. It reared up on its hind
legs, something no 'gator can do, and it was bigger than our
local bears. I thought it might be a circus animal, but the owners
always report escapes immediately."

"Why didn't you tell me all this yesterday?"

Hernandez snorted. "Help you steal Andrea's story?"

"The devil save us from our friends!" Blood kicked a sheaf
of papers by Arneson's desk. "Out of a misguided sense of the
solidarity of womanhood...."

"Misguided!"

Between his moans, Collins began chuckling. Arneson had
wadded the towel against his stomach to staunch the bleeding,
but he was tempted to move it up and stuff it in the terrorist's
mouth. Instead, he turned and looked up at his superior.

"Didn't you two say something about being in a hurry?"

Hernandez stared down coolly at her junior. Arneson wriggled his eyebrows. "Bill's my conscience. Sometimes."

The vampire shrugged. "All right, Hernandez. Truce. *Now*
will you take me to Holroyd?"

"Since you ask so nicely, and you're obviously anything *but*
a reporter."

Hernandez removed a holster from her desk drawer and
fastened it to her belt. She emptied the automatic, replaced the
clip with a fresh one, and sheathed the weapon. From a peg-
board behind her, she snatched a ring of keys.

"We'll take the airboat," she said. "It's the fastest way to
travel in the 'glades. Bill, how quickly can you dress Cuardi's
wound?"

"Don't bother," Blood interrupted. "It's superficial. Bleeding's stopped already. You probably hurt more than I do, Bill."

Arneson nodded wryly. "That was some tackle you made. You're a lot stronger than you look."

"My high-protein diet. No hard feelings?"

Arneson shook his head. "It was worth it. This is the first time I've ever seen Lucy lose a fight with a man."

"Don't get any smart ideas, kid," Hernandez growled. "I'm not doing anything I don't want to do."

"You never do, Lucy. But sometimes it's hard to convince you that you *want* to do something."

"Wipe that grin off your face. When you've finished plugging up our friend, you'd better call Charlie Grimm and give him the details."

"I spoke to Grimm before I came here," Blood interrupted. "He knows about Rudge, and he knows I'm going to Holroyd."

"Ask Charlie to pick up this human trash," the ranger continued, "and give him any help you can. Shit, I guess you'd better call Rafferty, too, but don't say any more than you have to. What he doesn't know won't hurt us." Arneson nodded. He'd dealt with higher-ups before. He slipped the handcuffs from his belt and fastened one end around Collins's ankle, the other to a desk leg.

Hernandez moved to the rear door and paused, holding it open. "Cuardi? Your name is Cuardi, isn't it?"

"That's what I've been telling people."

"Well, come along, whoever you are."

Behind the station, the veranda had been extended out over a stretch of river to form a narrow wharf. On Blood's left, a motor launch was fastened to a log pile by thick, tarred rope. To the right, an equally thick rope led to something resembling a floating set of playground monkey bars.

The airboat's fiberglass platform sloped gently at the bow and stern, not unlike a rocking chair. Two leather-padded seats were supported above the platform by a lattice of steel bars, facing a huge metal box that housed the gears as well as steering poles for emergencies. The stern was dominated by a steel cage the width of the boat. This encased the giant airplane propeller that powered the craft.

Hernandez clambered up the steel frame and perched inelegantly in the control seat. She pointed at the other, looked down at Blood, and said, "That's yours."

The vampire hesitated. The airboat did not sit flush with the wooden planking, and he could see green water flowing beneath his feet. Running water.

"My, ah, sea legs leave something to be desired."

"Oh, for Christ's ...! All right, give me your hand. Come on! I'm not the India rubber woman!"

Blood leaned forward as far as possible. His fingertips brushed the ranger's. He could not stretch his arm to reach her, for a transmutation in light of day meant being blasted to dust. If only the seats were lower!

Blood rose on his toes at the very edge of the wharf. He could sense the wooden ends splintering underfoot. But it was enough. The touch of her palm was hot. She strained to pull him aboard. Perspiration streaked her dark face. Blood could not help, for it took all his effort to hold on and keep from toppling into the stream.

Suddenly it was done. Blood was off the dock and wholly aboard. He let go at once, to the ranger's relief, and climbed easily into the passenger seat. He awaited the inevitable cutting remark.

Hernandez surprised him. "Are you sure that wound isn't serious? Your hand felt like ice."

He shook his head.

Her eyes narrowed. "You're not going to be seasick?"

"I just have poor circulation."

"Well, then, this will get your blood racing."

Hernandez turned the key in the ignition. The propeller started to hum behind them. Bending sideways, the ranger untied the anchoring rope and tossed it to the wooden planks, where it struck with a satisfying thud. She sat up straight and shifted a gear.

The propeller roared with sudden life. Boughs bent under its force. In seconds the airboat tore down the river, half out of the water, churning foam and screaming like a banshee.

"Exhilarating, isn't it?" Hernandez yelled over the rattling howl. Her cropped black hair flew straight back as the craft skipped over waterways at full throttle. Her face was exultant. She peeked at her passenger from the corner of her eye, and her grin spread wider and wider.

Blood clung grimly to the leather cushion of his seat. There were no safety bars to prevent his being flung off if Hernandez made a sudden, unexpected turn.

She seemed to make an awful lot of such turns.

EIGHTEEN

Surrounded by a meter-high sea of sawgrass, the Holroyd slave quarters stood stark against the stands of cypress and mangrove that encroached on the failed farmland. Brush cover was thinnest along the hummock's river shore. The score of men staking out the building kept to the thicker timber in a long, straggling line that extended from the narrow, muddy land-bridge that had enabled them to approach silently, on foot.

Crouched at the forward end of this line was a Viet Nam war veteran using the name Hemmings—sometimes Croft or Bullen, but usually Hemmings. Peering through field glasses, Hemmings could pick out his commander squatting in the tall grass at the other end, nearest the isthmus. Beside the white-skinned, bloated Snow was Robert, who'd been given Sleet's status to the amazement of the entire Free Thought Alliance.

The post was the same as Sleet's, but the job certainly was not. Were he alive, Sleet would be sitting where Hemmings was now. Robert was too young to handle a strategic position, and unblooded. It was he who'd turned away, revolted, when Farmer started to work on that sheriff. The sneer on Snow's face had not escaped Hemmings or Collins. Robert's moment of glory would be brief.

Being second-in-command meant little within the Alliance, anyway. Pecking orders were useful for performing minor tasks or delegating authority, but Snow never hesitated to reassign work when ability counted for more. Not like the way it was in the army, Hemmings mused bitterly, where commands went to chickenshit colonels fresh out of ROTC. Hemmings was at the front because he was the most seasoned of the three disaffected veterans in the Alliance.

The view through the glasses confirmed that Snow was no more inclined to move in now than he'd been twenty minutes ago, or when they'd first arrived. Hemmings wondered what Snow was waiting for. Farmer had scouted the building and returned without incident, but a second scout was still out. He did not question Snow's decision, of course. Just wondered.

He let the glasses dangle from his neck strap and unclipped the walkie-talkie at his belt. He licked his lips before speaking into it.

"Hemmings to Snow."

Static. Hemmings counted slowly to twenty before he transmitted again. Snow disliked impatience in his troops.

Sixteen. Seventeen. Eighteen.

"Snow here."

Hemmings moistened his lips again. "We may have company, Snow. There's a faint hum, like an electric motor, from the direction of the river."

Snow grunted. "I hear nothing."

"You're further away, and upwind. Request permission to send two men to investigate."

Static again. Hemmings could almost see Snow's lips moving in and out as he pondered the situation.

"Granted," crackled Snow's reply. "But they must be back in half an hour."

Snow switched off the walkie-talkie without waiting for an acknowledgment, and handed the mechanism back to Robert. "A good man, Hemmings," he said to his second-in-command. "Always thinking ... but not too much."

"Yes, Snow," Robert replied, refastening the clip to his belt.

Snow rested a pudgy hand on Robert's shoulder. He waggled his sub-machine gun in the direction of the ruins.

"There is a symbol of what we fight, Robert. Burn it into your mind. It will sustain you. The symbols of today are more subtle. People are cowed by the paycheck rather than the whip. It is no less slavery. By destroying such symbols of materialism we free the world from the insidious shackles of its monetary system.

We may be outlaws now, but one day the people will rise up. They will recognize the forces we battle as the true outlaws."

Snow's fingers dug painfully into Robert's deltoids. The youth nodded quickly. He failed to see how this goal could be attained by today's action, or last night's cruelties, but Snow was his leader. The leader sees further than anyone else.

"Collins is long overdue," Robert said softly. "And Chavez should have been back by now." One of his tasks was to bring such details to Snow's attention, but he did so with trepidation. The leader did not appreciate interruptions. Fortunately, the speech had been concluded for the moment.

"Yes, he should have been back." Snow turned to the shaggy-maned man on his left. "I hold you responsible, Farmer, if harm befalls Chavez. That you'd located the girl was enough, without your embellishment."

Farmer shrugged. He was used to Snow's temper, having been with the Alliance for eighteen months. As long as he went along with him, the pale man eventually relented. Sometimes that happened too late for the relentee, but some mistakes couldn't be allowed to slide.

"I saw what I saw." That was the extent of Farmer's defense. He lifted his field glasses and focused on the building in the clearing. "Maybe I should have handled the snatch instead of Petey," he continued, changing the subject. "He's not very bright."

"He's loyal," Snow replied harshly. "That's more important. As it happens, we don't need the ranger bitch's knowledge of these ruins, after all. The layout is less complex than Sleet's description. We could have razed that place to the ground and retrieved our high card by now if Chavez hadn't insisted on confirming your absurd report."

"I saw what I saw," Farmer repeated softly.

Robert cleared his throat. "You didn't have to let him, Snow."

Snow smiled thinly. "Considering what Rodicio has sacrificed for our cause, he's entitled to special treatment. Maybe it's better this way."

Farmer spared a glance at his leader, but said nothing. He understood Snow very well. Robert did not.

"What's better this way?" he asked.

Snow scowled. "I warned you about questions, Robert. If Chavez isn't back by the time Hemmings's men return, we'll move in."

Robert's jaw dropped. "But he might get caught in a crossfire!"

Snow silenced his second-in-command with a look from his ice-blue eyes, and began to picture Hemmings in Robert's place.

NINETEEN

The vampire tongued his retracted canines, assuring himself they had not yet rattled loose. The rushing wind tugged at his slicked-back hair, and river spray dotted his pale face.

"How much further?" he shouted over the motor's roar.

"You can see the hummock now!" Hernandez yelled back. She took a hand from the wheel to point straight ahead. "But we'll have to make a few more turns to get closer to the ruins!"

Blood reached forward suddenly and turned the ignition key, killing the motor. The great blade at their backs quickly stilled, but inertia kept them drifting at a goodly clip, angling towards the shoreline.

"What's the big idea, Cuardi?" The ranger snatched his hand from the controls. The unearthly chill of his flesh sent a tingle through her fingers.

"This overgrown toy makes enough noise to wake the dead, and I'll vouch for that any time. There's a small army of terrorists on that island. Remember?"

"Damn," Hernandez said softly. She bit her lower lip. Her eyes fixed on the muddy bank, which slowly drew the airboat to it like a magnet. The swamp was never still, but the birds in the hummock seemed particularly agitated. By the sound of their motor, or by the presence of several armed men?

"Damn!" she repeated, loudly. She turned in her seat to slam a fist against the propeller cage. The metal frame rang dully. "How stupid of me! We should have poled for the last kilometer or so!"

At least *you* could have poled, the vampire thought sourly. The act was a little too close to the volitional crossing over

running water for him to have been much help. The best he
could do was arrange for a breeze in the right direction. "It isn't
worth breaking your fingers over," he told her.

"It's unpardonable," she returned grimly. "I was enjoying
your discomfort, instead of thinking ahead."

Blood turned to her with a thin, not entirely unpleasant
smile. "Even when you make a mistake, it has to live up to your
standards, right?"

Hernandez could not hold back a laugh. "Damn right!" she
admitted with a grin. Then: "Brace yourself!"

Squitch! The airboat gouged itself into the bank sideways,
the side on which Blood was seated. The platform drew a thin
line in the soft ground. Blood clambered quickly onto shore, in
case the boat vibrated loose and drifted back again.

"Stay here," Blood ordered. "I'll do the scouting."

The platform rocked as Hernandez rose to follow. "I'm coming with."

"No."

"Don't pull that 'no place for a woman' shit on me, Cuardi. I
can take care of myself."

The vampire sighed. "I know you can. You don't have to
keep proving it."

"Sometimes I do," she said as she pocketed the key. "For
instance, when I've made an especially dumb blunder." She
paused, clinging to the framework, waiting for him to step back
out of her way. He didn't.

"Making a second blunder isn't the way to do it, Hernandez,"
he explained in an avuncular tone. "You know how this con-
traption works. I don't, and we don't have time for lessons.
Chances are very good that when we leave, it'll be in a hurry.
If you're already on the boat, you can start it up the minute you
see me coming."

Hernandez climbed back onto the platform. Her arms were
getting tired, and it was hard to talk reasonably with a man
when you were dangling your ass in front of his face. "Andrea
will need my help. She'll trust me up front, whereas you'll have
to persuade her."

"I persuaded you to bring me here," Blood pointed out.

Then his mouth hardened. "Andrea Blanchard is almost certainly dead. We both know that."

"We *don't* know that at all!" Feeling a tightness at her throat,
the ranger leaned over the platform edge and spat into roiling
water. Her ebony hair was not too short to fall before her face,
and as she pushed it back she turned to Blood again. Her hard,
dark eyes studied his gaunt form from scuffed boot toe to sal-
low face. The hole in his shoulder didn't seem to bother him at
all.

"We don't know it," Hernandez repeated softly, "but it's far
more likely than not." She sighed. "All right, Cuardi, hog all
the fun while I warm my tail and provide free lunch for every
bloodsucking creature on the hummock."

"A tempting offer," mused the vampire, lifting an eyebrow.
Before the ranger could ask what he meant, he added, "You're
not getting off that easily, you know. You may have to prevent
sabotage or keep some would-be soldier from giving an alarm.
Of course I've seen you use that automatic on your hip."

"Ninety-eight out of a hundred at my last proficiency exam,"
she said with pride.

"Don't make any noise unless you have to. And don't hesitate to take off if the odds go against you. You'll do more good
sending for the cavalry than lying face down in a sinkhole."

"Your concern is touching." She frowned. "Wait a minute,
Cuardi. Where's *your* gun?"

Blood pointed a forefinger in her direction and cocked his
thumb. Then he seemed to melt into the brush. Hernandez
stared for a long moment at his boot prints in the muddy bank,
already filling with seep-water. She realized her mouth hung
open only when a horsefly landed on her tongue.

Blood reached the edge of the central clearing quickly, and
moved only slightly less quickly on hands and knees through
the sawgrass sea. In the glare of day he could not transform
into a wolf's shape, but he could still use his wolf's cunning. He
followed the wind as much as possible, so that the grass bent
under him in the same direction. The creatures of the island
did not betray him with squeals and rustles, for he retained his
vampiric rapport with animals, especially rodents. There were

eyes watching, alert, somewhere on the hummock; he could sense their presence. But he saw no one, and he knew he was unseen.

The slave quarters was the only standing structure on the island, and an obvious base for the Free Thought Alliance. If for some reason they were *not* within, it would serve the vampire equally well.

The barracks-like structure had two long walls, but only one held barred windows. Blood approached the other, blind, side. A segment of this wall had crumbled, leaving a hole from the eave of the roof to a point just above the height of an average man's head. One man could squeeze through that gap, if he was very thin, and tall enough to get a solid grip.

In a single fluid motion, the vampire stood erect and hauled his slender body inside with a predator's stealth. Not a pebble scraped free to plink on the hard-packed interior floor.

He stood, knees slightly bent, in a narrow, unlit corridor that ran the length of the building. The breached wall behind him formed one side, and the other was lined with doorways, one for each of the cells in which Ben Holroyd confined his illicit cargo. Over the past hundred years some of the doors had rotted and collapsed, and through these sunlight arced toward the vampire. Some doors had survived, however, or perhaps been restored by hunters seeking maximum shelter with minimal effort. Thin slits of light along the edge of the corridor floor betrayed them.

There was a sharp tangy odor of oil and kerosene in the building, which drove out the pervasive Everglades aroma of rotting vegetation ... but there was a moldering undercurrent even more disturbing. The building was occupied, then, and a small generator had recently been used within its walls.

His boots trod noiselessly on the rough dirt floor.

There was no door on the first room Blood came to. It was filled with a jumble of electrical equipment. There was little sign of rust or age, but the arrangement—or lack of it—indicated the items were in storage. There had to be more such equipment in active use, or why the generator?

Blood frowned. None of this looked like anything the Free Thought Alliance would stockpile. An arsenal, or a bomb factory, would make sense for a terrorist group, but unless they were planning to electrocute their victims in the future ….

The next three rooms had intact doors. Blood passed them by. He'd be able to hear if a door opened behind him. First he wanted to be sure no attacker would leap suddenly from an open portal.

A woman moaned.

Blood stopped and spun around. The corridor was empty. He returned to the last door he'd passed. His pale fingers touched the rough, pitted wood.

The hinges were thick with rust, and the bolt casing only slightly less so. Blood jiggled the bolt gently, pulling it free by centimeters, a slow but nearly silent method. Rust flaked onto his hand, bright orange against colorless flesh. Blood made no more noise than a spider scuttling across a sheet of paper, and he was displeased at being even that loud.

His hand froze the moment the bolt slid free of its eye.

Slowly, again, the vampire pulled the door open, poised to halt at the slightest creak. There was none. The hinges looked rusty, but their pivot pins had been recently oiled.

He entered the cell, closing the door behind him.

The woman sat cross-legged on a soiled mattress against a side wall. Her hands were bound together at the wrists and held above her head by a length of bicycle chain looped through a steel eye imbedded in the wall. Her jeans were tattered shreds below the thigh, and there was barely enough blouse to tie over her high breasts.

It was not easy to reconcile the haggard cheeks, dull eyes, and slack jaw with the brightly beaming face in the photograph on Arthur Blanchard's desk, but chin and nose and ear shape did not lie.

Sunlight streamed through a narrow barred window, the sill of which was half a head above Blood's hairline, to strike Andrea Blanchard full in the face. Her head was, in fact, turned to receive its warmth on her tightly-drawn flesh. The brightness prevented her from seeing her visitor clearly, but something—the slight breeze of the opening door, perhaps, or the faint fetor that clung to the vampire—told her he was there. She moaned again, and her dull eyes grew moist.

"Oh, God, already?" she sobbed.

Blood moved forward, avoiding the battered broiling pan that obviously served as a chamber pot. Apart from exhaustion, which might have been largely psychological, Andrea Blanchard seemed to be in good physical shape. Too good, in fact. Blood couldn't help noting that her hands boasted a full complement of five fingers each.

Why would Arthur Blanchard lie to him about that finger in his desk?

"Please," Andrea continued, "please don't do this. Don't take my arm. I can't stand any more. Let me alone; let me die."

Blood stepped into the stream of sunlight, his neck muscles tensing at its touch. "I'm here to help you, Andrea."

The woman's eyes flickered with surprise as they took in the cadaverous form. Then she dropped her chin to her chest and stared at a greenish stain on the mattress.

"Oh, great!" she muttered. "Now I'm hallucinating. Next I'll start talking to myself. Damn it, Andrea, you *are* talking to yourself! This place is a haven for loonies."

Blood reached forward to lift her chin. She flinched at his cold touch.

"I'm no hallucination, Andrea."

She sniffed. "You're not a fantasy? You're a real live human being?"

"I'm as ... real as you are."

The dullness began to fade from her eyes, replaced by suspicion. "How do you know my name? Who are you? How did you get in here?" The eyes narrowed. "Do I know you?"

"Wouldn't you rather talk somewhere else?"

She almost permitted a smile. "By all means, let's get out of here. My questions can wait."

So can mine, Blood added silently. For a little while. He fingered the chain. "They wanted you to stay put, didn't they?"

Andrea grimaced. "That's my own fault. First he used a rope. I've got strong teeth, but I was too anxious to wait for the right moment. He came back before I could chew through the last strands."

Blood nodded and grasped the chain on either side of the eye. At night, he could have snapped these flimsy strings of metal between two fingers. His human form retained much of its abnormal strength, but lacked a vampire's relative invulnerability. He could easily over-stress his body.

The tiny links pinched the skin of his palms, sliding and tearing, even drawing a drop of blood. "I need better leverage," he said. "Can you stand?" Andrea straightened her legs. Her ragged fingernails found cracks for holds in the rough wall. Blood gripped her elbow and helped haul her erect.

"Wouldn't it be easier to find a pair of pliers?" she asked as she saw his scored flesh.

"I'm not very good with tools." The chain now had enough slack for Blood to wrap it around each hand. Standing in front of the prisoner, his chin almost touching her forehead, Blood suddenly yanked in opposite directions with all his strength.

The chain held.

"I know where he keeps…." Andrea began.

"Quiet."

He yanked again, to no apparent effect. The third time, however, he saw one of the links twist under the stress. He gave the chain a final yank.

The link popped, and the chain parted, its ends clanking on the hard-packed floor. Suddenly freed, Andrea staggered against the vampire. He caught her left arm and held her steady until she regained her balance. With his free hand he quickly unwound the chain from her wrists.

Andrea leaned against the wall, studying her rescuer with renewed interest. His grip was icy, but of course her arms would tingle numbly as circulation returned. She rubbed them vigorously.

"That's some trick," she said, her voice shaking. "You must be the life of the party."

"The death, actually."

"What?"

"I'm no good at small talk, either. Can you walk?"

She laughed sharply. "Mister, I'd crawl on hands and knees to get off this soggy island … and away from that damned thing!"

Blood's eyebrow rose, but he said nothing. Time for questions later, as agreed. Lots of time. Lots of questions.

Supporting Andrea with an arm about the waist, Blood led her into the corridor to retrace his steps. He boosted her up to the breach in the wall, and she didn't have to be told to climb through. He heard a soft groan as she landed outside, but she otherwise held her tongue. Blood was glad of that. He'd had to rescue far less sensible people. When he followed, though, he was disappointed to find her standing as she waited for him.

The vampire dropped down in a crouch, and pulled her down beside him. "Do you want to be seen?"

Her forehead wrinkled. "By whom?"

"Guards. Patrols."

"He doesn't need guards," she explained.

"*Him,* then!"

Andrea swallowed hard. She leaned heavily against Blood's side, then recovered her footing. "No," she breathed. "No. He spends his mornings stealing oranges and setting animal traps."

"Keep your head down anyway. This is my rescue. We do it my way."

"You're the hero," she said with a shrug. "I'm just the distressed damsel. As long as we get out of here fast."

Blood agreed.

They had just crawled out of the shadow of the former slave quarters when the first burst of gunfire ripped through the air.

TWENTY

Deputy Charles Grimm was living up to his name. A scowl etched his leathery face, accenting the flaccidity of his jowls, and his eyes were icy marbles. He resented being called away from the strategy meeting. Captain Peter Miranda of the Highway Patrol had arranged space for him in their headquarters while a forensic team worked on Sheriff Rudge's office, and Grimm appreciated that, but he wished the desk sergeant had been ordered not to disturb them.

He slapped open the door to the reception area and glowered at the gray-haired man in uniform seated behind the desk. The sergeant, used to passing on undesired messages, merely nodded toward the young man thumbing through a wall display of wanted flyers.

"Davies?" the deputy growled.

Davies sized up the speaker coolly. "Who are you?"

"Charlie Grimm, acting sheriff. You asked for me by name. I'm pretty busy, so if you'll state your business ...?"

Davies nodded briskly. "I know you are, Sheriff. That's why I'm here." He flipped through a card case until he found what he wanted, and held it out for Grimm's inspection.

The deputy's eyebrows crawled up his forehead. The hard lines of his lips formed a toothless grin. "Well, that *does* make a difference. You should've told the sergeant."

"Security precaution." Davies quickly put his card case away. Until he'd seen what a hard nose Grimm was, Davies wasn't sure he'd use it; now he was glad he'd never turned in his FBI identification. Funny, how readily the Bureau believed him when he'd said he'd lost it.

"We were just about to call your Miami office," Grimm said, leading Davies down an apple-green corridor.

"Oh?"

"We can handle most local problems, but from what I've seen and what Bill tells me I think we're out of our depth."

Davies nodded, his eyes hard with what he considered steely resolve. "Yes, indeed. I stopped at your office before coming here." No point in adding, Davies decided, that he'd mistaken the rustic building for a roadside diner. "I've run up against these same slime before, Sheriff, and it was no picnic."

"Deputy," Grimm corrected. "I may be acting for Paul Rudge while he's being patched up, but I can't fill that man's shoes."

"Loyal, eh? I like that." Davies grinned, enormously pleased with himself.

"It's the plain truth." Grimm stopped in front of a conference room and opened the door. "We're here."

A score of men and women were seated at or standing near a long wooden table in the center of the room. At the head of the table, a detailed map of the Everglades had been propped on an easel. Telephones were so arranged that one or more would be within reach of anyone at any time. Grimm escorted Davies to the map and addressed the gathering.

"Gentlemen, ladies, this is Allen Davies of the FBI. He's here to help in this unusual situation."

Davies started to smirk, then decided a sardonic look was more appropriate. Such an expression befitted a leader.

Grimm indicated a man in a park ranger uniform, who sat on Grimm's right and seemed not much younger than Davies himself. "This is Ranger Bill Arneson. He works for Lucy Hernandez. They captured Peter Collins, who we believe was involved in the assault on Paul Rudge."

Collins? "I'd like to talk to this Collins," Davies said.

"We all would," Grimm replied, "and we will as soon as he's out of intensive care. Lucy shot him."

Davies scanned the table. "Which one is Lucy?"

"At the moment, Ranger Hernandez is on Holroyd

Hummock with a reporter named Al Cuardi."

Davies raised a disapproving eyebrow. "A reporter? This is no place for amateurs, Sheriff."

"I don't think he's really a reporter, Mr. Davies," Arneson put in.

"I was talking to your sheriff," Davies hissed.

"Deputy!" Grimm snapped.

"Sheriff," Davies countered. "I've promoted you. But you'll have to do something about discipline. You, ranger, get up. I'm taking that chair. You probably shouldn't even be in the room." That'll show them who's running this show.

Arneson stood and stepped back a pace. Grimm looked ready to explode, but the ranger caught his eye and shook his head slightly. It wasn't important enough to argue about.

Grimm took a deep breath and continued. "Cuardi had called me earlier to tell me about Paul Rudge, but he refused to come in. A pair of orangemen saw him leaving the sheriff's office, and we've got them going through our mug files in case he's someone we know about already."

Davies jerked a thumb at Arneson. "The kid's seen him, too, hasn't he? Why isn't he with them?"

"Because," Grimm growled, "he has far more information, and we need him here."

Davies shrugged. Sometimes you had to be flexible.

"On your right, Davies, is Captain Peter Miranda of the Turnpike Troop." The deputy spoke staccato.

Davies turned and smiled. "I've read your warning many times, Captain."

Miranda soaked up the weak banter impassively. "Yes. Very droll, Mr. Davies."

"And on *his* right ..." Grimm continued.

"All very competent, I'm sure," Davies interrupted, in a tone that conveyed the opposite, "but I'm not interested in a bunch of names I'll forget almost at once. The important thing is that everyone here knows me. I'm taking charge of this operation, and as long as each of you jumps when I say jump, we'll get along fine. Social amenities waste time. Minutes count!"

"We know that, Mr. Davies," Captain Miranda replied,

before Grimm said something everyone would regret. "I've put every man I can spare on this case. I've also telephoned the governor. National Guard units will be ready in half an hour. We can't move in on Holroyd Hummock until then, but as soon as I get the word...."

"I haven't had lunch," Davies said suddenly. "Your wastebaskets are full of paper wrappers, and I haven't had my lunch yet."

Arneson spoke from behind Davies. "There might be some corned beef left. I'll see."

"Thanks, Bill," Grimm replied. "Better hurry. We haven't much time for ... amenities."

Davies seemed oblivious to the dig. "Corned beef?" he exclaimed. "I can get that at home, any day. I want something indigenous. I want an ... alligator-burger." He turned to Arneson with a smile.

The ranger looked back with wide and disbelieving eyes. Then he shrugged. "There's a tourist trap on route 41 that makes them, but it's a twenty minute drive. Frankly, Mr. Davies, they don't taste all that interesting."

"Damn. All right, corned beef, and a tall glass of freshly squeezed orange juice."

"Er, that's a bit scarce, too...."

"In Florida? I ought to report you to Anita Bryant!"

"Yes, sir, but most people prefer the consistent flavor of frozen concentrate. Fresh-squeezed can be sweet one time, sour the next."

"Skip the lecture, Bill," ordered Grimm. "Just do what you can."

Arneson looked sheepish. "Sorry, Charlie. Reflex. I spend most of my time explaining things to visitors." He turned quickly to leave the room.

"And Key Lime pie!" Davies called after him.

The door slammed shut.

"Kid's got a chip on his shoulder," muttered the man from Washington. He noticed the others watching him closely. An attentive group. Good. He rubbed his palms together in anticipation. "Now, Sheriff, just where *is* Holroyd Hummock?"

Grimm leaned back and jabbed at a red circle on the

easel-braced map. The paper wrinkled under his thumb. "You don't even know that, Davies?" he growled. "Just how long have you been in this state, anyway?"

Davies glanced at the black band on his wristwatch, then changed his mind about pressing the digital readout button. An accurate answer was not called for.

"That doesn't matter. I'm here because I've had personal experience with the Free Thought Alliance."

"Surely they could have provided you with a local man," Miranda pointed out.

"No one was free." Davies continued rubbing his hands together, but the knuckles were turning white. He didn't like being put on the defensive.

"Too busy to help capture the most dangerous group of terrorists in the country?" Miranda's eyes popped slightly.

"Cuardi said the FTA was at the top of the Bureau's list," added the deputy.

Davies licked his lips. "Cuardi's an asshole. Our Miami office is tied up tracking down illegal aliens—one of the local problems you don't seem to be handling very well, Sheriff! That's why I have to rely on the support of everyone in this room to get the job done. If I don't get their co-operation, heads will roll!" Ha, he thought, that got their attention! He continued in a calmer voice. "Now, as I understand it, you're planning to send a squadron of men to one small island in the middle of a vast swamp based on the fourth-hand report of a man beaten to the point of delirium."

Grimm reared up, his eyebrows lowering. "You listen to me, Mr. FBI. I've worked with Paul Rudge for twenty years, and I'd sooner believe my mother unreliable. I'm not about to take a chance of losing a single one of those bastards. The people in this room have spent most of the morning working out an attack plan, and a damned good one, too!"

Davies rose, facing Grimm eyeball to eyeball. "You needn't raise your voice, Sheriff. We can't afford emotional outbursts. I know how you feel about what happened to Rudge. I was one of the Alliance's victims myself, and consider myself lucky to be alive."

"You?" Grimm's anger melted, transformed into mixed awe and pity. "Like Paul?"

Davies nodded. "I'd rather not talk about it. The point is, we have to be a thousand percent sure the Alliance is there, and *then* pour in everything we've got! Captain Miranda, get Goodyear in Miami on the telephone."

The Turnpike Trooper blinked in astonishment. "Goodyear? As in tires?"

"As in blimp. I noticed their airship on the way here. It's perfect for reconnaissance."

"We have helicopters."

"The Alliance would hear them and scatter like rabbits. Anyway, I've always wanted to fly in one of those things."

Miranda grunted. He slid his chair back from the table and struggled to his feet. "Men's room," he announced.

Deputy Grimm caught the urgent look in the captain's eye. "I'll go see what's taking Bill so long."

"Don't take too long," Davies warned. "I won't explain my plan twice." The two men walked together down the corridor, their heels clacking on the tiled floor. Miranda paused at an alcove and bent his head to the water fountain.

"If Davies really was tortured by the Free Thought Alliance, it must have affected his brain," Grimm said.

Miranda wiped a trickle of water from his chin. "Charlie, have you ever worked with the feds?"

The deputy shook his head. "Paul's talked to a few of the agencies. I once did legwork for them on a smuggling case. I wouldn't call it working together, exactly."

The captain nodded. "Well, I've met a few government men who seemed regular enough, which means you don't mind too much when they get credit for solving a case you did the preliminary work on. Others are arrogant glory-grabbers. They'll come down hard if you cross their plans, intentionally or not. They're secretive as hell, but God help you if you hold out on them. And those are their good points."

Grimm sighed. "You're telling me to grin and bear it?"

"Not exactly." Miranda folded his arms across his chest and leaned against an apple-green wall. "Something doesn't sit right about Davies. I think I'd better give Commissioner Weinberg a call."

Grimm licked his lips hungrily. "You think you can get Davies yanked off the case?"

Miranda raised a cautioning hand. "Don't get your hopes up. It may take hours to cut through *all* the red tape. But I think so, yes."

"Hours." Grimm grimaced. "Those terrorists aren't going to wait for us. I don't know which is worse: arguing with Davies, or going along with his harebrained scheme."

"That's why you're not going back in that room with me, Charlie." Miranda lowered his voice. "I'll make your excuses and keep him out of your hair. You get my men and those National Guard units into position. We want them ready to move in the minute Davies is removed."

A slow grin spread across the deputy's face. "Jeez, Peter. I really owe you for this! I hate to stick you with him, though."

Miranda shrugged. "I'm used to this crap. You'd probably pop him in the eye. Your face was redder than a baboon's ass."

"Yeah. Oh, I'll need your authority."

"I'll arrange it now."

Grimm's brow furrowed. "What if we can't get Davies pulled off?"

Miranda sucked on a front tooth before replying. "In that case, you and me are in a bodacious amount of trouble, son."

TWENTY-ONE

Snow ripped the communicator from Robert's grasp before the echoes of the shots began to fade.

"Damn you, Hemmings!" he yelled into the transceiver. "I gave strict orders: no gunplay before my signal!"

Static gargled in response. From the veteran's end of the line, however, came a blood-curdling scream. It was all the more horrible for its abrupt end.

"I can't see anything," Farmer complained. "Those trees are screening it."

Snow snatched the binoculars and tossed the walkie-talkie aside. Robert had to lunge to catch the communicator. The leader pressed the glasses to his eyes and roared "Hemmings!"

Rifle fire continued; if anything, it increased. Between bursts came the shrieks of more men. Dying men.

"Where is that disobedient traitor?" Snow muttered. "I just want to see his face one last time."

There! Something moved, between those mangroves! Snow tried to sharpen the focus, but the shape remained blurry, a dark brown mass like an upheaval of earth. Then it was gone.

"Robert! Are there earthquakes in the Everglades?"

Robert dried his hands on his khaki trousers. "I don't ... Jesus Christ!" Where the mass had stood a moment ago, a soldier leapt from concealment. No; he was flung. No man would jump so high to land head-first in the clearing. Snow could see the gap in the sawgrass where the body sprawled. The soldier did not rise.

Snow flung the glasses to the ground. "Enemy attack!" he yelled. "Assault on Hemmings's flank! Take the offense!"

Alliance troops eagerly broke cover and rushed toward the sounds of death. The action was a welcome break from the morning's tense waiting. A handful of their number might be taken by surprise, but nothing short of a platoon could stand before the alerted might of the Free Thought Alliance. Even a platoon would be hampered by the terrorists' hit-and-run tactics.

Snow charged into the fray avidly, though his weight slowed him down. He wished only that he could have changed places with Hemmings, so as to lead the attack physically. Robert trotted alongside, deliberately holding back to keep pace. Farmer lost seconds in retrieving the binoculars, but quickly took a two-meter lead.

Farmer stopped cold in his tracks. "Holy shit."

Snow's brown mass stepped into the clearing.

The creature stood three meters tall, with shoulders more than half as broad, and resembled an enormous, ambulatory mud pile. The skin was a series of dark, scaly patches, beneath which an occasional streak of raw pink or crimson flashed, and apparently clumped together by thick, heavy mire. Arms were elongated, like a gorilla's, so that knuckles scraped the ground. Legs were disproportionately short and massive. The round and liquid eyes, seemingly all pupil, reflected a malevolent intelligence that even a self-absorbed fanatic such as Show could sense.

The thing had broken cover to finish off an Alliance soldier trying to crawl away. An enormous hand covered the man's face and jerked the head back. Snow could hear the spine snap.

Then the creature plunged back into the trees.

"It's prehistoric!" Robert gasped.

Farmer had watched the killing through his powerful field glasses. He lowered them carefully into their case and then stood perfectly still, his rifle hanging slack in his left hand. His voice sounded hollow.

"It's true. There *is* a skunk-ape."

Snow came up behind Farmer and slapped a broad palm between the man's shoulder blades. Farmer staggered forward to retain his balance, and let the momentum carry him onward. Greenery blurred before him.

"Idiot," Snow spat.

"Farmer's right," Robert said, forgetting who he was contradicting. The air smelled of rotting meat, bad eggs, kerosene.

Ten automatic rifles emptied their rounds into the mobile, oozing mass. Many bullets, fired in panic, went wide, but many more struck home ... to no effect. Two Alliance members were hit by ricocheting or ill-aimed bullets, but the monster barely flinched under the steel-jacketed onslaught. It plowed through the rapidly dissolving line. Its wake was littered with weapon men dead or dying, with broken necks or crushed limbs.

A black youth saw his best friend's skull crack open beneath a huge foot. Enraged, he leapt at the creature, stuffed his .38 Smith & Wesson into its belly, and emptied the clip. The thing staggered ... for a moment. Then the avenger was lifted into the air and shaken like a kitten until his bones cracked. The corpse was discarded as casually as an orange peel.

With more than half their number destroyed in minutes, the remaining soldiers gave way. But the creature's stride was greater, for all its bulk and misshapen limbs. One man after another fell, leaving a trail of gore.

Snow suffered agonies at the sight of his army—*his* command—fleeing like whipped dogs. "Kill him, you worthless scum!" he screeched. "It's a trick! It's a man in a costume!"

"No," said Robert.

Snow turned his piercing, deadly eyes on his aide. "How dare you? In a crisis, dissension cannot be tolerated!"

Robert was too numbed by the violence of the skunk-ape's attack to be cowed by a menacing look. "It's not a man. We can't kill it. It's like shooting mud." Robert pointed at a straggling soldier forced to make a stand. The man was firing his automatic rifle as quickly as he could pull the trigger. They were near enough to see the line of bullet holes appear on the creature's right arm ... and disappear as rapidly, for the dark skin seemed to flow over the wounds, sealing off tricklings of rust-colored blood.

The monster did not pause. It tore a great mangrove root out of the ground and used it to crush the shooter's skull.

"A good trick," Snow admitted. "I'd like to see him try it

after my grease gun cuts him in half!"

Farmer continued forward blindly, stumbling into the thing's grasp. He did not even try to use the rifle. He did not even have time to scream.

Robert tugged at a thick, fatty arm. "Snow, we have to retreat while there are still a few Alliance members left!"

Snow raised his sub-machine gun. "No."

"Snow, we either leave or we die!"

"No retreat. Can't you see it, Robert? This monster is a symbol of materialism, sent to test our resolve. It is the personification of power. It cannot be slain piecemeal. We must kill it completely, and we must do it now!"

"There's no way!"

"I have a plan." With his free hand, Snow urged Robert toward the advancing creature. "Lure it into my range."

Robert dug his boot heels into the soft mud. He turned defiantly. Snow's icy blue eyes held less terror for him now.

"That thing will kill me as it killed Farmer."

"Not if you're fast. Anyway, I'll avenge you. Your name will live in glory, Robert. To die for our cause is a great honor. Look at what Rodicio gave up for us!"

"To die for a reason, to make a point, yes! Rodicio tried to sacrifice his life to protect the Alliance and take some pigs with him. But nothing can be accomplished here! What will our cause mean if we're all dead?"

Snow swung his weapon to point at the young man's stomach. "You're disappointing me, Robert. Do as I order, or I'll put an end to your whining." Robert stepped back a pace from the corpulent man. He was going to die. His mouth became dry. His hands shook with fear, with anger, with betrayed faith.

"Now I see what you really are, Snow. You don't give a shit for the cause, except that it feeds your swollen ego. You're no brilliant tactician, nor the first of a new breed of supermen. You're just an old-fashioned demigod! A megalomaniac! You're insane!"

Snow's eyes turned cobalt. His trigger finger tightened. "The world is insane, Robert. Not I."

Robert turned to run. Show's gun chattered. Burning

needles stitched the aide's body, ripping though lungs and throat. The bullets missed his heart, but three buried themselves in his brain. Half of his head was blown away. Robert was dead before he hit the ground.

Snow shook his head sadly. "A waste," he muttered. "But he couldn't be relied on. The Alliance, like the rest of the world, needs purification. The evil must be cut out and eradicated."

He looked across the corpse-strewn clearing. Two pairs of survivors struggled toward him, desperately striving to avoid the creature's grasp. They were all that remained of his glorious Alliance. The rest had proven by their failure to be undeserving. Four men and Rodicio Chavez if the latter still lived, if the creature had not slain him first. It was enough to rebuild with.

If these four were worthy.

"You men! No retreat! This is the most important battle of all! A turning point! You must fight on for the Alliance! We *can* win! We *must* win! We *shall* win!"

The four men seemed to falter. They saw Snow raise his weapon. They saw Robert's bleeding corpse.

But they heard the awful tread of the skunk-ape growing nearer, and the only way off the hummock was past Snow.

Fools, thought Snow. Still retreating, despite my orders, in spite of my encouraging words and—greater betrayal!—the cause to which they had dedicated their lives. How little those vows meant now! The symbols of materialism must be faced down and smashed, not run away from.

One soldier read Snow's intent and lifted his own rifle. He was too slow. Four bursts from Snow's sub-machine gun purified the Free Thought Alliance.

The creature turned and dodged into a stand of cypress.

Snow laughed. "You've seen what this chopper does, eh? I can turn you into hamburger with this baby. Come a little closer. Let's see how fast you can die. That's it, out of your hole."

Snow moved into range like a gunfighter in an Old West shoot-out. When he was near enough, the gun chattered again, spending its full force on one of the trees, splintering its trunk.

The creature roared, threw its weight against the tree, and

dropped. Its putrid flesh melded with the muddy ground. The cypress creaked and groaned before toppling, snapping in two where rapid-fire bullets had torn through it.

Snow cheered and fired at the ground where he'd seen the creature fall. Another roar of pain filled the air.

"Got you, you slimy bastard!" Snow was exultant. Panting heavily, he moved in to confirm the kill.

Amazing, Snow mused, that so bulky a being could all but vanish in the trampled mud and sawgrass. The coloration was excellent camouflage, of course, and it must have learned patience in order to trap prey. Not that it needed any special skill to remain still now. It was dead. It had to be dead. Snow's victory tasted all the sweeter because he alone had remained true to the tenets of the Free Thought Alliance.

Then he saw the thing, and halted. Hadn't it fallen further to the right, about two meters? Did it still live? Had it crawled so far?

He raised the gun. It would crawl no further.

In the few seconds it took Snow to raise the muzzle, the monster rose, wrapped its arms around the fallen cypress, lifted the trunk from the ground and hurled it through the air. The machine-gun spat, but the monster was a blur, and dodged easily. Snow went down under the tree's crushing weight. The weapon expended itself harmlessly into the air.

Snow was pinned on his back, writhing under the crushing burden across chest and shoulders. His right hand was pressed between the now useless weapon and a thick branch. The fingers were too mangled to squeeze the trigger again.

Yet it was outrage, not pain, that shone in his ice-blue eyes as the creature lumbered forward.

"Decadent symbol of materialistic excess!" Snow spat, flecking his lips with blood. "You cannot defeat the Alliance. There will be others. New names, new techniques, but the same dedication to freedom! Purification is inevitable. You can...."

The creature's misshapen mouth worked to form two slurry but unmistakable words.

"Shut up."

A huge, muddy hand engulfed Snow's round face. The

struggle was brief. The fat man's attempt to use his teeth only hastened his suffocation.

Absently, the creature pried loose Snow's machine-gun. His wide, brown, liquid eyes passed over the bloody clearing and focused on the barracks-like slave quarters. Then, swinging the dead man's weapon like a walking stick, the monster shambled forward.

TWENTY-TWO

"No guards, eh?" said Blood. With that final machine-gun burst, the fighting seemed to have ended. He was not entirely reassured by the thought. The Free Thought Alliance was involved—it had to be. But it was too soon for Grimm to arrive, so who the hell were they shooting at? With the barracks blocking their view, Blood had no way of knowing. At least that factor had helped them reach the cover of the trees unscathed.

Andrea Blanchard sat with her back supported by a thick cypress trunk. Her hands lay limp in her lap. "I guess the Alliance finally decided to come get me."

"Finally? A little too soon, for my tastes." He offered her a hand. "We can't stay here, and there's no need to, now that we don't have to dodge stray bullets. The longer we wait, the more chance there is of being spotted by the Alliance."

Andrea struggled to her feet. "Maybe they lost."

"In which case the survivors will shoot you on sight." He noticed that her knees, scraped and bleeding from scrabbling through the sawgrass, were trembling. "I can carry you."

Andrea shook her head. "I'm not ready to collapse yet. Just tell me where we're going."

"Along the riverbank. Hernandez is waiting with her airboat."

"Lucy's here?"

"Down that way. She'll get you to safety and see you get proper attention." He offered an arm for her to lean on. She waved it aside.

"Just me? What will you be doing?"

"I'm not sure yet. Finding out what the shooting was all about, for one thing. Come on."

At first, the only sound was of their progress through the marshy undergrowth. The woman's progress, anyway, for Blood moved with a predator's stealth. Then a limpkin called tentatively to its mate. A small rodent flashed across their path, rustling the grass. Something splashed in the river, though the trees obscured their view. The swamp, startled into silence by the heavy gunfire, was coming back to life.

When Blood judged they were within a few meters of the boat, he risked breaking cover. The hummock's bank sloped sharply at this point. The airboat was not in sight. Nor had Hernandez seen him from some new hiding place, or she'd have turned on the motor at once.

Andrea came forward to stand beside Blood. The cool displeasure evident in his face made her uncomfortable.

"Lucy was here?"

"I thought so." Blood moved nearer the water. Suddenly he knelt in the mud. "Yes. These are my tracks. She must have had to move on. Maybe she thought they were shooting at me, and went for help."

Andrea sat at the edge of the river and bent forward to wash the bloody scratches on her arms and legs. She cupped cool water in both hands, then stiffened. The water dribbled from between her fingers, unnoticed.

"Oh god," she whispered.

Blood hurried to her side.

Andrea's face, already pale from captivity and deprivation, drained to ash-white. With a shaking finger, she indicated a silvery gleam amid the roiling current. Sunlight reflected off the top bars of a propeller cage, just centimeters below the surface. The rest of the airboat was hidden by muck sinking had churned up.

Blood scooped up a handful of mud and crushed it in a hard, dry lump. "No sign of a struggle. Maybe she got away."

"And maybe she's who they were shooting at. Oh, god, Lucy."

Blood the cynic surprised himself by asking, "Are you always so cheerful? That was a hell of a lot of gunplay to down one woman."

Andrea shrugged, staring into the river. "The Alliance thrives on excess. Besides, I've had damned little reason for optimism lately. The question is, how do we get out of here now?"

"On foot. It means circling around to the other side of the hummock." He smiled thinly. "Ready to collapse yet?"

Andrea started to rise, tucking her feet beneath her. But the left foot slid in the mud, and the right leg refused to lift. "Looks like it," she admitted.

Blood circled her shoulders with his left arm, slid his right under her knees, and lifted. Her arms went around his neck for additional support. Again the woman was startled by the chill of his skin, but she had as little faith in her senses as in anything else these past few days. She was probably anemic, not him. She'd be surprised if she were not.

"Tell me when I get too heavy," she said.

"Then I'll take over," came the thick, slurry voice behind Blood.

Andrea glanced over the vampire's shoulder. Her whole body tensed. Sobbing, she curled tighter against Blood's chest.

"It's not fair," she moaned.

Blood turned slowly to face the speaker. He recognized at once that here stood the reason for the excessive gunfire that had echoed across the hummock. His nose confirmed the reason for the creature's popular name.

No one had mentioned it could talk.

"Mister Skunk-Ape, is it? Or do you prefer something less formal?"

The creature cradled a sub-machine gun in its right arm. The muzzle waggled at them. "That was quite a diversion you arranged. But not good enough. Your friends are dead."

Friends? The Alliance! "All of them?" asked Blood.

The mouth seemed to grin. "All."

"Damn."

Blood ignored the gun. The skunk-ape's fingers were plainly too thick and blunt to use it. That it possessed the weapon at all, though, and had survived an attack by a well-equipped group of fanatics, was proof enough of a deadly opponent.

"Do you live around here?" asked Blood.

"My laboratory," the creature replied, waving the gun in the direction of the slave quarters. "I insist you stay for dinner."

Blood adjusted the weight of the woman in his arms. Mercifully, Andrea seemed to have fainted.

"As long as we aren't imposing."

Blood marched toward the clearing. The creature followed closely.

TWENTY-THREE

"Damn you!" swore Andrea Blanchard. "You raised my hopes for nothing ... again!"

Blood ignored the jibe. The woman had to vent her frustration somehow, and he wasn't exactly pleased with this turn of events himself. He jangled the thick chains that fastened him to the cell wall opposite Andrea, testing them, repeatedly stretching them full length and letting them fall slack again.

Andrea's new bonds were equally heavy. She preferred conserving her strength, although to what purpose she could not say.

"You're wasting your time," she said. "That's no rusty bicycle chain you're playing with. It's tempered steel."

"I'm testing the wall clamp," Blood explained. "There must be more than mortar holding it in place. Ben Holroyd didn't want his merchandise to roam very far, I gather."

Andrea grimaced. "Holroyd was a saint by comparison."

Blood fingered a thick link. The weld was solid. He'd have to stress the metal itself to make it snap, and he couldn't get the proper leverage in his position. Even then, he wasn't sure he could manage it by day. He had to wait for sunset.

"Tell me about our host," Blood said to Andrea. "Has he always looked like a walking dungheap, or is that some esoteric cure for acne?"

Andrea looked up at the vampire and sighed. His chain was much shorter than hers, forcing him to stand. At least she still enjoyed the dubious luxury of sitting on the evil-smelling mattress.

"I suppose you think that's funny."

The agent shrugged. "I warned you about my small talk."

The woman shivered. "I don't want to talk about him."

"That's understandable, Andrea. But one reason we were caught was that I didn't know what I was up against. Any information you give me will mean a better chance of success next time."

"Next time!" She stared up at the pitted ceiling in exasperation. "Don't tell me about any next time. If I had a dollar for every time I thought I was getting out of one mess, only to end up in a worse one ...!"

Blood waited.

"His name," she said at last, "is Lionel Parker. He says. He was a biological researcher for a pharmaceutical house in Norfolk. Then the accident happened."

"What kind of accident could do *that*?"

Matted brown hair fell across Andrea's forehead. She rubbed against her upper arm to push it back. "The way he looks now is his own doing. A car crash crushed his legs below the knee. He returned to his job, but began neglecting the company's projects to work on his own."

"Which involved what?"

The reporter bit her lower lip. "Regeneration." She took a deep breath before continuing. Her chains scraped the plaster wall. "When the company clamped down, he used his insurance settlement to buy equipment and silence, and set up this laboratory. His experiments with small mammals were so favorable he couldn't resist trying the process himself. It worked, but there were side-effects."

Blood fixed his gaze on Andrea's left hand. All five fingers looked normal, from where he stood. "I see he's since perfected his technique."

Her eyes widened. She wriggled her fingers. "You know about that finger?"

"I saw it."

Her head thudded softly against the rough wall. "My father sent you. Why didn't I think of that before? Too bad Parker's formula doesn't seem to do much for brain cells."

Blood smiled thinly. "You did have other things to worry about," he pointed out.

"At least you got further than the other one did. If Daddy keeps sending people, I may be home by Easter. If I live that long. If there's enough of me left then."

"You're talking about Frank Jordan."

Andrea nodded, and stared at the mattress.

"What happened to him?"

She swallowed back bile. The cell had always had a rank, moldering odor, but it seemed worse this afternoon, probably because she'd had a taste of fresh air. "Dead, if he's lucky. Otherwise, he's in one of the other cells. You may be moved in with him when your turn comes."

Blood's voice took on a chill he'd been suppressing. "Why didn't you tell me there were other prisoners?"

The woman fought an urge to cringe. "Hey, mister, you didn't want to chat, remember? I really don't know whether he's alive or dead, or for that matter what happened to the Alliance guy Parker grabbed along with me. I don't encourage Dr. Parker's conversation. His shop talk isn't very pleasant."

On the other side of the cell door, a bolt scraped free. The door swung open abruptly, halting the discussion. The gap was quickly filled by a monstrous form that seemed to ooze out of the corridor darkness.

Parker had to bend to avoid striking his head against the lintel. His bulk seemed to fill half the cell as he lumbered in. Scaly brown flesh covered Parker's body, flapping in loose folds. Pale yellow fluid seeped from his joints. A dirty strip of adhesive tape held a particularly pronounced plica to his forehead so it would not cover and possibly grow over his right eye. The fingers of his left hand were obscured by the handle of a wire basket of fruit, but the right showed two stubby digits among the usual five. The feet also boasted more than enough toes, including rudimentary ones that stuck out at the ankle like a rooster's spurs.

Parker's flabby, oversized lips pursed out when he spoke. "Getting acquainted? I thought you two knew each other already. Would you really go to such lengths to rescue a stranger, Mr. Cuardi?" He lifted the basket, displaying its yellow-orange contents with pride. "I've brought lunch. Variety is limited, but

Miss Blanchard can tell you I set a generous table."

"I'm not hungry," the vampire replied.

Parker smacked his lips. "Don't let the color put you off. What you see at the market has been subjected to a chemical gas to bring out that bright orange color. It has nothing to do with taste. Once an orange is picked, it stops ripening."

"The pips get stuck in my teeth."

The massive right shoulder churned, shrugging. "I'll leave them anyway. Even without an appetite, you may get thirsty. I trapped an alligator last night, so we'll have steaks for dinner. It's very good, properly cooked. Like chicken, but with more flavor." His liquid gaze focused on Blood. "Or would you prefer yours raw, Mr. Cuardi?"

So Tom hadn't been imagining things last night. Blood's lips thinned. How much had Parker really seen? How much did the doctor understand of it? But the agent held his tongue.

Parker stepped toward the woman. Andrea shrank against the rough wall to avoid his touch, but the loathsome fingers never came near. He merely set the basket beside the mattress, within her reach, and then moved back.

"You might as well eat, Miss Blanchard," Parker said with a note of resignation. "I've apparently denied you breakfast for nothing. With all this excitement, there won't be time today for your next operation."

At the last word, the reporter shuddered and fixed her gaze on the crack between wall and mattress. Sourness filled her mouth, and her arms were starting to tingle from lack of blood. *Her* arms; the original equipment. She strove to ignore Parker's insensitive words and noisome stench, to imagine herself in another time and place. But her mind could not wholly deny the body's shackles.

"I wonder if anyone else is looking for you, young lady? You're almost more trouble than you're worth. The others never attracted such attention."

Blood swore silently. He had to distract Parker from that line of thought. Grimm would have a tough enough time when he got here without the biochemist setting a trap for him.

"Miss Blanchard has told me of your work," the agent said.

The misshapen face seemed to glow. "Has she?"

"Restoring her mutilated finger was a remarkable achievement."

"Child's play," Parker replied in a tone belying modesty. "Literally. Children as old as eleven have regenerated fingertips past the first joint. I merely restimulated Miss Blanchard's natural ability. A weak solution of my serum, and a slight augmenting of her normal bioelectricity, was all she needed."

"Without anesthetic," Andrea added harshly.

Parker glared at the woman. "Local pain killers block the serum's effectiveness. The pain isn't that bad. I bore a greater agony to restore my legs!"

"You were a willing subject!" she spat.

Blood grimaced. He could understand the woman's bitterness, but he wished she'd sulk in silence. There was a chance the vampire could hypnotize Lionel Parker, but he required his captor's full attention.

"Scientists have worked with bioelectricity since Galvani's time," Blood said, "but what's this serum you mention?"

The hulking form turned back to Blood with glee. Parker rubbed skull-sized hands together, warming to his subject. "It's a trade secret, and still not perfected. Fingers are a snap. When entire limbs are involved, complications set in."

Blood's feral eyes caught and held Parker's liquid orbs. "Please continue," he said, ignoring Andrea's groan.

"What happens," Parker replied, "is that the body's resources are taxed beyond their limits. The process involves grafting the patient's own ependymal cells to the stump, and humans have few of those to spare. With the aid of my serum and voltaic boosters, body electricity breaks down the graft into undifferentiated blastemal cells. These in turn transform the normal cells they touch. New cells and old multiply together. When they reach their limits, they differentiate again to reproduce the missing limb."

Don't turn away, Blood thought. "How do you control the growth?"

"Ah, there's the difficulty, keeping the cells from differentiating too soon. My methods can restore a finger in a couple of days, even without ependymal cells. An arm takes two weeks. I still can't produce sufficient cell growth at the amputation site to form a complete limb before differentiation. When I retard the process, the cells die, unable to metabolize fast enough to survive."

"And how long did your legs take?"

Parker offered a lopsided grin. "I see what you're getting at, but you see the side-effects. I was pursuing a different line of research at the time, studying the ability of lizards to regenerate tails, feet, and so forth. That was why I chose the Everglades to work in. I would break down the constituents of lizard cells, mix them with my own DNA, and ... but I'm giving away my secrets."

Yes, Blood thought, your secrets. All of them. "What went wrong?" he asked, funneling his willpower.

Parker's eye-ridge lifted. "Nothing serious. I didn't regulate the serum properly. The lizard cells assimilated mine and kept growing. They still are, but at a slower rate, since they're running out of directions. They love a good wound. Gives them a chance to show what they can do. I can heal the most horrendous injuries in seconds without leaving a scar."

"Or any trace of humanity," Andrea put in.

Blood welcomed the interruption, this time as an excuse to cease the mental effort. Parker was too self-absorbed to respond to ordinary hypnosis.

"Humanity!" sneered the biologist. He leaned toward Blood like a California mudslide. His tone became conspiratorial. "She brings up that humanity tripe every chance she gets. I know better. Do you think I'm trapped in this shape? I know exactly what happened. I could reverse the process any time."

"Why don't you?" asked the vampire.

"Why should I? This body is very useful. She'll change her mind when she has more first-hand experience."

"He's loony!" Andrea shouted. "He wants to cut off an arm just to see if he can grow another there."

Parker waggled a blunt finger at her. "Don't exaggerate, girl. It's just the hand, this time." He turned back to Blood. "This is why my other experiments were less successful, Mr. Cuardi.

I tried to do too much at once. When I saw how well Miss Blanchard recovered from her minor loss, incurred under less than sterile conditions, I realized that the human body had to be acclimated to this ability, as only certain specialized organs are used to it naturally. First a finger, then the hand, then the forearm perhaps to the elbow. Joints can be tricky."

"That's enough, Parker," Blood said.

Parker glanced at the reporter. His lip sagged in disdain, and a moist noise came from his nostrils. "Yes, she's been a disappointment. I wish she had more objectivity."

"Your shop talk would make Jack the Ripper squeamish," the vampire continued. "Anyone but a glorified tadpole could understand that."

"Glorified tadpole!" Parker drew himself up to full height, scraping the ceiling with his thick, lumpy skull. His massive hands clutched air by the fistful. "Bah! You're as incompetent as she, Cuardi! A real journalist would appreciate the scientific importance of my work!"

"You're the one with the blind spot, Parker. You're only playing at science. Your research has potential, but you'd rather work on freak show tricks!"

A rush of air puffed out the oversized lips. "Freak! Show! Trickery! Glorified tadpole!" Stooping, Parker ducked out of the cell with an undignified lurch. Wood chips scattered as he slammed the door and rammed its bolt into place. "Tadpole!" echoed in the corridor, only slightly muffled.

Blood shook his head slowly.

Andrea gasped for air, unsure whether to sob with fear or break out laughing. "You shouldn't bait him. He might decide to saw us in half."

"I got rid of him."

"I appreciate that. I'd've appreciated it more if you hadn't gotten him started. What worries me is that he's starting to make sense." Andrea stared at the door, ears pricked, hands clenched. After a moment, her fingers relaxed. "He's going out."

Blood nodded. He heard the heavy fading footsteps himself, far clearer than she could.

The woman smiled wryly. "His process works better than he

thinks. My vaccination scar is gone, and my jaw hurts because a new wisdom tooth is pushing out a bridge."

Falling silent, Andrea Blanchard plucked an orange from the basket. She peeled it methodically, devoting full attention to the mundane task. One by one, she separated the segments and raised them to her lips to suck juice from the pulp.

Blood took advantage of her temporary distraction to withdraw mentally. What he did was not exactly telepathy, but it was a step beyond ordinary mesmerism. By concentration he could communicate with and control, with his superior will, creatures traditionally associated with vampires ... and influence many other species. His mind searched the tall grasses for a suitable messenger, and quickly fixed on one. The animal balked, tried to bolt. The vampire's will clamped down like a steel trap.

Instructions were conveyed, simple ones. Look. Listen. Remember. The tiny mammal would obey, dared not do otherwise. Blood only hoped for a swift return. Whatever plans were being made by Deputy Grimm and his associates could have a bearing on the agent's own strategy.

Blood opened his eyes and looked again at his fellow prisoner. The peel of a second orange was falling into her lap. Andrea Blanchard had kept her sanity through the horrors of kidnapping, abuse, and mutilation, and the inhuman Parker with his peculiar theories and terrifying promises. An admirable woman, but still human. Terror, pain, despair, and fatigue were wearing down her body and her mind. Tonight's escape had to succeed. Another letdown might push Andrea over the edge of madness.

Neither he nor her father had expected to find her alive and whole but, since she was, the agent was obliged to deliver her safely. To do less was to fail his trust.

Blood hated to fail.

TWENTY-FOUR

Rodicio Chavez huddled low along the outer wall, almost directly beneath one of the high, barred windows. He hardly dared to breathe for fear of rustling the concealing sawgrass. The sun blinded his single eye when he looked to the bloody clearing, but he needed no reminder that the noble social experiment of the Free Thought Alliance had been thoroughly crushed.

He'd sat through the slaughter in numbed dismay, staring at the stumps of his wrists. What purpose could he serve now? Martyr to a non-existent cause? Inspiration for a field of corpses? No. He could look forward only to a lifetime of pity and condescension.

His thick lips set in defiance. He would not submit to the largesse of a society that he despised and had tried to destroy. He'd rather die. Truly he would. All he'd had to do was stand and draw that creature's attention, and he'd be slain as readily as the others.

It was one thing to wish for death, and another to wish for that sort of death.

It was well he had not done so, he now thought. When he'd first reached this spot, he'd sat in the mud and pouted for almost an hour, like a child. He wanted to see with his own eye what Farmer had reported. But Farmer had scrabbled up the rough wall to peer through the bars. Chavez could hardly do that.

When the fighting broke out, he stayed there out of fear. Afterwards, he remained partly from shock, partly because there was nowhere else to go. He'd seen the creature, and the strange pale man, and Andrea Blanchard, as they returned to the ruined slave quarters, but he could not get a good look at the woman's left hand.

Still, he heard enough of the conversation that followed to tell him that Farmer had spoken the truth. Andrea Blanchard's finger, the very finger Rodicio Chavez had watched Snow cut off while relishing her screams, had grown back, in a matter of days! And the miracle-worker was the monstrosity that had wiped out *his* comrades!

Chavez watched Parker's gray-brown hulk stumble toward the scene of carnage, probably to clean up the mess. The terrorist struggled to his feet and started toward him. Carefully. He had to talk to this man, or whatever he was now, and he naturally didn't wish to be killed first. If Parker rejected his proposition, then all hope was gone and death would be welcome. But if it were accepted ....

Chavez had believed in the Alliance's cause for what it could do for him. Even crippled, he held a place of power in the order. Parker had proven himself superior to the Alliance, and Chavez saw no conflict in offering his loyalty to the new cause of scientific research. His price seemed fair enough. A pair of hands. His own hands.

TWENTY-FIVE

Two pairs of boots trod the veranda of the ranger station. Weathered boards creaked under the weight. Keys jingled until one was singled out. It slid easily into the government-issued lock, and turned with a click.

Poised to climb a leg of Bill Arneson's desk, a brown rat stiffened at the sharp sound. She stifled a distress squeal, but her ears and whiskers twitched. Humans approached. Every instinct told the rodent to flee, reinforced by the distance from her home territory.

A more powerful will overrode her fear.

She raced from the desk to scamper up the nearest wall. The rough wood offered ample grip for her long, pink toes. From there she leapt atop a file cabinet and settled behind a stack of folders and manila envelopes. From this hiding place, she could see and hear almost everything that transpired. She even had a fair view over the top of Hernandez's partition. The animal did not have to comprehend; merely remember. The one who sent her would pluck the significant details from her subconscious.

The door swung open.

A heavy-set man in uniform entered first. He had a sour expression on his face. A silver badge glinted on his chest. His cool gray eyes scanned the interior quickly and professionally.

"Could be bigger," he said. "Miranda will be sending us more help when he can, and of course the National Guard will be here soon."

A younger man in a different, darker uniform followed. He had firm round cheeks, a snub nose, and hazel eyes. "I could take down that partition, Charlie," he offered.

"Don't bother," Grimm replied. "We'll only need this space for a few hours. I hope. Where can I sit?"

"Use my desk." Arneson lifted a stack of disordered papers and piled them without ceremony atop the folders on the file cabinet. The rodent froze in a mock-dead position. Panic coursed through her veins. But she did not betray her presence.

Grimm settled into the polished wooden chair and reached for the telephone. The steady dial tone extracted an approving grunt. He dialed the number Miranda had given him.

"I'm glad you thought of coming here, Bill. With Davies lording it at the Highway Patrol, and Paul's office shut down, we really need a central headquarters."

Arneson smiled shyly, pleased at the compliment. "It's also closer to Holroyd Hummock."

"Speaking of which, see if you've got a detailed map of that area while I'm waiting for Commissioner Weinberg's buddy in Tampa to pick up his damned telephone!"

Arneson opened a middle drawer of the cabinet. The rat jerked, then backed against the wall, hoping to remain unseen. A rhythmic buzzing suddenly pulsed through her rump, but she had enough experience of people-dwellings to recognize it. The cord of Arneson's telephone ran from the desk down along the wainscot, and then up inside the wall behind her. The vibrations presented no danger to her, and would add to her subconscious store of information.

As if cued by Grimm's outburst, the ringing stopped and a gruff voice snarled in the deputy's ear. "Walt Conklin."

Grimm gave Arneson the high sign. "Mr. Conklin, good morning. My name is Charlie Grimm, and I'm...."

"I know who you are. I spoke with Carmine half an hour ago. Do you have more data for me?"

"Ah, no, sir. I was wondering how you were getting along."

Conklin made a deep, throaty sound. "I don't normally get involved in this sort of thing."

"I understand, sir, but this is an emergency."

"Carmine wouldn't ask if it wasn't," Conklin snapped. "I asked the Bureau in Miami to call back twenty five minutes ago."

"This *is* rather urgent, Mr. Conklin."

Conklin sighed. "All right, Grimm, stay on the line. I'll call again and you can listen on the three-way. Keep your mouth shut."

"I'll be quiet as a mouse."

Grimm clapped a meaty hand over the speaker and nodded for Arneson to unroll a surveyor's chart across the desk. Guidebooks and paperweights and even Grimm's pistol were used to hold the map flat. Arneson awaited further orders.

Grimm looked up at him. "You make me nervous, standing there. Pull up a chair and listen along. Then I won't have to repeat it all."

Arneson complied with the eagerness of a puppy. He tried to put on a solemn face, befitting this trust, but his eyes shone with pride and excitement.

A new voice came on the phone, thin and nasty, like a pregnant mosquito's whining flight. "Yeah?"

"I don't believe it," Conklin said smoothly. "Hank Breid answering his own telephone."

"Walt? That you?"

"I left word for you to call me, Hank."

"I saw the message. I was getting to it."

"When? Next Tuesday?"

"That's not fair, Walt. I'm up to my receding hairline, trying to get a line on last week's rash of brutal robberies down here. Our new image, you know."

"I thought you'd have that sewed up by now."

"Not that easy, Walt. These punks popped up out of nowhere, and now, for no reason, they've disappeared again. We need a new angle, and there isn't one."

"Is that why you sent Allen Davies to Paul Rudge's jurisdiction? To look for fresh angles?"

"Who?" asked Breid. "Every man on my team is working the Gold Coast, and I'm already over budget for the fiscal year."

"Allen Davies," Conklin repeated. "Says he's from Washington, so he might not be regular staff. Sure you didn't request help from the head office?"

Breid snorted. "For days I've been requesting help, without

effect. How about his bona-fides?"

"Apparently in order."

"Hell. Be just like those bastards to send a man to the wrong place, and not tell me besides. I'll look into it."

"That's just for starters," Conklin said. "I want him out."

Breid whistled. "I haven't the authority."

"But you know who does. You know me, Hank. I wouldn't ask this if it wasn't essential. Davies is lousing up a local operation and endangering lives. He's got to be pulled."

"If I had a nickel for every local law enforcement agency who bitched about the Bureau wrecking its plans ..."

Conklin cut in. "It's not jealousy, Hank. These people want help. They *asked* for it. What they got was Davies. You know as well as I that even the FBI makes mistakes."

"Who made you watchdog, Walt?"

"Who made you God?" Conklin answered softly.

Breid sighed. "All right, I'll do what I can. I'll take your word that Davies is a flake, but if I catch any flak.... "

"I appreciate it, Hank. Call me when you've got something. Or call Captain Miranda direct, since he's wet-nursing Davies."

"I said I'll do my best. Tell Miranda not to hold his breath." Breid slammed down his receiver hard enough to make both Grimm and Arneson wince.

Conklin kept the line open. "You still there, Grimm?"

"Heard every word. How much of it was true?"

"All, I think. Hank Breid is too good a liar to come up with such a thin story. He really doesn't know Allen Davies."

"How long will it take?"

Conklin grunted. "You heard the man. Don't hold your breath. I'm going to try some of my Washington contacts, too, but no promises."

"Can't ask for more. Thanks." Grimm hung up the telephone before adding, "for nothing."

Arneson wiped a sweaty palm on his slacks. "If we wait too long, the terrorists will be gone long before we get to Holroyd. They may have already left."

"You're not telling me anything new, Bill." Grimm rubbed the back of his neck to ease the knot of tension building there.

Long, leafy shadows streaked the station's windows. It was late afternoon and Grimm was impatient. "They'll have trouble slipping past us by day. The Turnpike Troop'll be watching for them. We'll wait for dusk, then move in, Davies or no Davies." He licked his lips. "They can only fire me once."

"I'll make some coffee," Arneson said.

Grimm bent forward to study the map covering Arneson's desk. It draped over the edges slightly, crinkling when Grimm pressed his gut up close. After a moment, he leaned back, frowning.

"This covers too much territory, Bill. I need something more detailed, focusing on the immediate area. I want to know every stream and footpath the Alliance could use to get away."

Arneson opened a box of filter paper. "That's a tall order, sir. The last major survey was thirty years ago, and so out of date that ... wait a minute. We have a set of satellite photos taken last winter. They're not easy to interpret, but we could match them against the charts." Arneson dropped the filter paper box beside the coffee maker, stepped around the deputy and yanked open the top drawer of the file cabinet. The weight shift was too much for the unstable stack on top. Files spilled to the floor ... accompanied by a terrified field rat.

With a squeal, the creature scampered for the window it had entered by.

"Damn!" swore Arneson. He snatched a broomstick from the corner and gave chase. The ranger's first blow caught the tip of the tail, rewarding him with a shrill cry. He swung again, too soon, and missed. Before he could recover for a third attempt, the rodent was up the wall and through the torn screen.

Arneson slammed the window shut and stared through the rain-streaked glass. His prey had already vanished into the undergrowth. With a shrug, he left the broomstick on the sill.

The furry creature dashed through grass and ground vines as quickly as four feet could carry her. The crushed tail-tip throbbed, but the urge to escape overwhelmed even that agony. Anyway, she'd gathered as much information as she could absorb; now she had to deliver it. Once that obligation was discharged, she could return to her normal foraging lifestyle.

The animal scurried in a serpentine course, swerving to avoid tree roots, predator trails, and, not far from the station, a bedraggled figure stumbling along the ragged, twisting trail. These were minor, daily hazards, even the human, and so made no particular impression on her mind. The rat had no conception that the newcomer might be important, and as a result her information would be stale before it was delivered.

TWENTY-SIX

"Sunset at last!"

These were the first words from Andrea Blanchard since she'd reached for the first orange that afternoon. She'd finished seven or eight oranges since then, and distracted herself by forming patterns on the mattress with the peels and pips. She'd seemed oblivious even to the squealing, medium-sized field rat who'd stood on the high window sill not half an hour earlier. Of course, why shouldn't some rodent, scenting the fruit Parker had left, scurry up the rough outer wall to investigate? Why shouldn't it hesitate, finding the cell occupied, and then flee at the man's sudden head movement, which resembled a nod?

Blood shrugged off a feigned sleep and fixed his gaze on her through the gloom. She met his eyes steadily but passively. The chamber pot gave off a fresh, acrid odor; he'd pretended to doze while she used it. Soon she would begin to wonder why he did not also need to relieve himself.

Blood, too, had been awaiting the last light of day, though Andrea could hardly know why. She might suspect that he expected reinforcements, and she would be wrong. Grimm and the others were being unpardonably delayed. The woman's fate rested wholly with Blood, and the agent was satisfied with that responsibility. He disliked relying on frail humans.

"Sure you don't want an orange?" Andrea asked. "Sometimes he forgets dinner."

The vampire shook his head. "So you like the dark?"

She peeled another fruit for herself. "I never used to, particularly, but Parker usually prowls all night, looking for food or fresh victims. I don't think he ever sleeps. The replicating cells may not let him. It's just a relief to know that he's not under the same roof. At night I can close my eyes and pretend none of this is happening."

A cricket paused on the window sill, momentarily filling the dark, tiny cell with frantic chirps. Beyond, a panther's roar drifted on the twilight air. But the vampire's keen hearing detected no other movement within the former slave barracks. He wanted to complete scouting the interior for other prisoners. With a rescue party delayed, the longer Parker looked for Blood's non-existent allies, the better.

"You look tired, Andrea," he said softly.

"Exhausted. What did Parker call you? Cuardi?"

"He read it off my press card"

"Is it your real name?"

He smiled invisibly in the gloom. "Call me Al."

"I feel like a used dishrag, Al. I can only sleep for a few minutes at a time. I've been too scared."

Blood nodded, though he wasn't trying to make conversation. His words were a suggestion.

"You feel sleepy now, don't you, Andrea? Look at me."

The woman's dispirited, dark-rimmed hazel eyes met Blood's. The feral red glow in his orbs startled her. She felt she was being drawn out of herself. She tried to protest, but her jaw fell slack.

"You cannot keep your eyelids raised, Andrea," the agent continued softly. "You must rest, at least for a few minutes. Relax. Sleep."

The reporter fell under Blood's spell in less time than Sheriff Rudge had, now that night had fallen. She leaned back against the dank, moldy wall as if it were a well-stuffed pillow. Blood was pleased. Andrea *did* need rest—soon there'd be little time for it—but as his main purpose, Blood had things to do he'd rather Andrea did not see. Already she must suspect far more than any scandal-sheet writer ought to know.

Blood's shape began to quaver, melting slowly into a soft, gray cloud. His chains fell empty, clinking against the wall. He solidified a hand long enough to silence the bouncing manacle, and then the mist sank slowly, slowly, to the floor of the cell. It passed easily through the narrow gap between door and lintel.

Blood drifted waist-high along the narrow corridor. The doorless room next to Andrea's was crammed with still more electrical equipment. More than one piece was on the verge of rusting to uselessness. Beyond that was another door, unbarred and slightly ajar. It was unoccupied, but signs of fresh filth and a thick, heady mixture of sweat and excrement indicated it had not been so for long.

The next room was formed of two cells. Fragments of the dividing wall showed how crudely it had been knocked down. An overhead rafter sagged, robbed of its support. Here was another haphazard collection of machinery, but more organized and spread out. It smelled of recent, frequent usage; more than recent, for a soft hum permeated the room. Either Parker neglected to turn off his generators, or he deliberately let them run at low power to save warm-up time.

In the center of the double chamber, perpendicular to the missing wall, stood a metal operating table. It was draped with wires that led to nearby batteries. Rubber sheeting was spread over the damp rough floor as protection against shocks. Two more squares of rubber covered the high, barred windows. The flash of an electrical discharge could attract unwanted passersby.

Blood urged his loose-knit molecules forward through a setting that rivaled the movie laboratories of Doctor Frankenstein. Experts would have to catalog these instruments. Blood could only guess at some of their applications, though he sensed that much of what he saw was superfluous.

Something pulled at Blood, lightly but insistently, before he reached the exit. It was a force he'd never encountered before. He paused to investigate, allowing himself to be drawn to it.

The living mist shimmered and wavered. Too late, Blood recognized the threat. The agent had moved within range of an operating spark collector. The nearer he drifted to the collector, the stronger its grip on him became.

Blood cursed his own carelessness, but only for a moment. He engaged all of his monumental will power in a struggle to pull free. The mist-form was his weakest manifestation but it had also been one of his least vulnerable ... until now. If the spark collector sucked him into its workings, as it might in a matter of seconds, the mist would condense. The vampire's atoms would scatter, and he would not be able to regroup them because his consciousness, too, would be scattered.

Surprisingly, Blood felt no pain. When the time came to end his cursed existence, this might be the preferred method. But it was neither the preferred time or place.

By mental energy alone, he slowed his descent into the machine ... but slowed it only, not stopped it. He was trapped. The moment he'd entered the field, it was too late to metamorphose to a corporeal form that would be unaffected. Something of his substance would certainly be drawn into the collector even as he changed, and likely as not it would be something vital. The vampire healed with supernatural swiftness but he could not, as Parker claimed to do, regenerate limbs and organs. He must fight his way free as a mist, or perish.

The mist shimmied dangerously. Even trying to hold steady at this point might tear the molecules apart.

The agent's sole bit of luck was that the generators were set at such low power. Otherwise he'd have been sucked into the collector already. In fact, the power was too low to maintain a steady flow. There was a faint but perceptible pulse to it.

Even at the weakest point of the cyclic rise and fall, Blood was relentlessly drawn forward, but the pulsation gave him an idea. It required split-second timing, though, and Blood had to implement it at once. A few more seconds in the machine's grip would be his end. There would be no second chance.

At the next power peak, Blood not only ceased struggling, he pushed forward himself. The mechanism loomed suddenly, a voracious, living metal and glass monster.

It wasn't entirely painless, after all.

He was centimeters from the gaping maw when the thought came to him that he'd miscalculated, the power would not drop off when he'd estimated it would, the pulses were not as even as he'd assumed.

He should at least have removed Andrea Blanchard's chains,

and given her a fighting chance.

Then the force ebbed.

Having angled his approach, Blood used the momentum from the strong pulse to drag himself *past* the machine. Now, if it would only throw him far enough, fast enough....

The power surged, snatching angrily at his atoms. Blood strained forward. The mist seemed almost frozen in the air.

Almost.

At the next weakening, Blood floated free of the field. He was safe.

Mist could not sigh, but a vampire could, and did, when Blood resumed his natural shape. His dead white skin tingled from the near-fatal encounter. Muscles in his limbs and chest, normally quiescent, trembled. As far as Blood could tell, he remained a complete entity. He must have lost a few molecules—bits of skin and bone and hair—but apparently no more than living people lose every day, unnoticed.

Though the solid Blood was immune to spark collector's threat, he gave the machine a wide berth on his way out.

TWENTY-SEVEN

In the next cell, Blood found Frank Jordan. What was left of him.

Jordan lay supine on a mattress even filthier than the one in Andrea Blanchard's cell. A three-strand nylon rope circled both mattress and naked torso; the restraint seemed superfluous. A chamber pot near the man's crotch had overturned, fouling torn and faded fabric.

Inured though he was to horror, death, and inhumanity, Blood was revolted by Lionel Parker's handiwork.

Midway down the thighs, Jordan's legs ended in tiny, twisted feet that seemed almost dainty, like the feet of Oriental concubines of an earlier era. Web-like flaps of skin connected the toes. A pair of diminutive hands, resembling the paws of a baby chimp, sprouted from the shoulders.

Jordan groaned.

Blood hurried to his fellow agent's side, neglecting to shut the cell door behind him, amazed that the man still lived.

Jordan's right eye looked up at him. The left socket was almost hollow, save for a growth like a pale white pea in the center. He flapped his hands in agitation, a bizarre parody of a large flightless bird: the last dodo, left for dead by wild dogs more interested in the chase than in food. His lips moved, and his head twisted violently. The vampire knelt to catch the man's faint words.

"Who ... you?"

"It's all right, Jordan. Arthur Blanchard sent me."

The hand fluttering ceased. "Thank ... God." A puffy tongue pushed through his cracked lips. "Dry."

Blood glanced around the small, dark room, his excellent night vision picking out every detail. The only liquid was a thin slime retained in the chamber pot by its curved lip, but there was also another wire basket containing half a dozen oranges. The vampire did not bother peeling the one he grabbed, but simply held it over Jordan's mouth and squeezed. Drop by drop, so the man would not choke, Blood let the juice fall onto Jordan's eager tongue. Some of it spilled down the man's chin, attracting several flies with the sweet odor. The insects seemed not to bother Jordan—there were dozens alighting and crawling on his mutilated body—but Blood willed them all to leave.

"Thanks," Jordan said at last. His voice was raspy but stronger. "Do you know what's been going on here?"

"Some of it," Blood replied coldly. "Enough."

Jordan struggled to raise his head. "What about the girl? Have you seen her? What did that devil do to her?"

Blood gripped the man's shoulder with a pale hand. Cold as his touch was, the contact, any contact, would steady Jordan's nerves. His voice was edged with tightly controlled hysteria, understandable but dangerous. Carrying a quadriplegic through the swamp would be difficult enough by itself.

"Andrea's fine. Parker's only regenerated her severed finger, and hasn't yet gotten to his own experiments." Blood's lips thinned. "Nor will he."

Jordan sighed, relaxing slightly under Blood's grip. "Praise God! I don't know how clearly you can see what he's done to me, but I myself saw worse. Parker dragged in one of the terrorists along with Andrea. That man managed to kill himself, after which Parker decided to tie me down."

Blood's long, thin fingers tugged at the knot at the edge of the mattress. Parker's malformed digits were ill-suited for tying, and the strands came apart easily. Small wonder the biologist's operations were little more than crude acts of hacking away.

Jordan's body rocked. "What are you doing?" he asked.

"Taking you out of here."

Jordan shook his head violently. "I'll slow you down. Get Blanchard's girl out of this hell. That's what matters."

"I can't leave you here at Parker's mercy."

"You won't if you kill me first."

Blood ran a tongue over his razor-sharp canines.

"I'm not crazy," Jordan continued. "Not yet. But every day I get closer. Even if you got me safely away, what kind of a life would I have? Blanchard would pop for a generous pension, but my vulnerability makes me a security risk. Outside of my work, the only things I care about are hunting and fishing, facing the wilderness on my own terms." His eye filmed. Salty liquid traced a line through dirt and dried blood down the side of his head. "I *can't* kill myself. That's why Blanchard stationed me domestically. I wouldn't carry cyanide capsules."

"Everyone fears death," the vampire said quietly.

"You don't understand. I welcome death now. But self-destruction is the final, ultimate sin, the one transgression beyond absolution. If *you* kill me, you can confess and be absolved."

Blood's feral eyes widened in momentary astonishment. He wondered how a man with such scruples had ever gotten on the staff of the expeditious Office. But he had no objection to indulging Jordan. The man on the mattress wore no crucifixes or holy medallions, but Blood supposed Parker had confiscated them to prevent Jordan from swallowing one and choking to death. The symbols meant little to Blood, but their absence would simplify matters.

The vampire touched a finger to Jordan's temple. He felt the throb of blood rushing through veins.

"I can do it painlessly. You've made your peace?"

"I've had nothing else to do for days."

"Then relax. It's almost over, and you can sleep. Sleep."

Blood's voice droned. Jordan succumbed willingly, even gratefully. He did not feel the needle-sharp fangs pricking his neck, or the greedy sucking that distended his jugular. At one moment Jordan was unconscious, drifting in a dreamland he devoutly believed was prelude to the afterlife; in the next, he was dead.

When he was finished, Blood wiped his lips and lifted Jordan's corpse. Strange how light a man could be, shorn of his limbs, and how little blood there was in his stunted body!

He carried the body into Parker's laboratory and placed it on the metal operating table. Here, surrounded by metal and glass and sheets of treated rubber, Blood could safely use the decay-speeding bacteria to dispose of the remains. This wasn't entirely in accord with Jordan's religious beliefs, perhaps, but it was both a necessity and a mercy. Resurrection as a crippled vampire would be double torment to a man of his faith.

Blood withdrew a capsule, pressed it against the man's chest until it snapped open, and quickly removed his hand. A second's exposure to air activated the voracious microlife. As Blood stood there, a tiny hole appeared over the breastbone. It spread rapidly. In an hour, Frank Jordan would be only a name.

It was at that moment that Blood decided Doctor Lionel Parker had to be destroyed, not just imprisoned.

As if to underscore the agent's resolution, a sudden burst of gunfire echoed from outside the slave quarters. The agent moved to one of the windows and drew back a corner of the rubber curtain. He saw nothing of interest. The shots came from a different part of the hummock than the site of that morning's slaughter.

Since Blood expected no help from the authorities this soon, Parker must have been mistaken about slaying the entire Free Thought Alliance. Either one or more terrorists had escaped and brought back reinforcements, or the Alliance had had a back-up force standing by to move in at dusk. The result was the same: Parker would be kept busy. This time Blood would take full advantage of the distraction.

He wasted no time returning to Andrea's cell. Not even pausing to draw the bolt, Blood smashed down the door. Metal hasps dangled by rusty nails, and wood splintered against the opposite wall.

Andrea slouched in peaceful slumber, just as he'd left her. He braced one foot against the wall, above her head, and yanked. The chain stretched its full length, resisting his great strength. Then the eye ripped from its wall mooring. White powder rained down on the reporter, and some fragments clung to Blood's slick black hair. His powerful fingers curled under her wrist manacles and pried them open as easily as peeling a banana. He threw the links behind him, knelt before the woman, and snapped his fingers.

"Wake, Andrea," he said curtly.

The woman revived with a start. She immediately began rubbing her prickling arms to restore circulation, and brushing plaster dust from her ragged clothes. She stared into Blood's inexpressive face, trying to orient herself. The sound of gunfire from outside added to her puzzlement.

"What's that? Another of your tricks?"

Blood helped her quickly to her feet.

"I wish it were my doing. That's probably more of your Alliance playmates. Isn't it nice to feel wanted?"

She stared suddenly at her wrists, with wide red marks where the manacles had pressed against the flesh, and then at the shattered wall behind her. "How the hell did you manage that? I've seen strong men snap bike chains, but this stuff!"

"It's all leverage."

"And how did you slip loose from your chains …?"

"We don't have time, Andrea." He pushed her roughly through the shattered cell door, hoping she wouldn't ask about that as well.

"Are we going to look for Frank now?" she asked.

"No," Blood snapped. "You were right. Jordan's dead. Now get going before Parker decides to look in on us."

That got her moving. "I just wish one of these damned rescues would take."

TWENTY-EIGHT

Earthbound shapes stood silhouetted against the moonless night sky. The blackness was attenuated by distant lights of civilization and the first smattering of stars. To Andrea Blanchard, the darkness seemed both limitless and unbearably confining.

Blood tugged at her arm, hurrying her along. Andrea knew that, if he chose, this strange pale-skinned man could dislocate her shoulder. She discerned only his aquiline profile and the faint red glow above his nose, and wondered if his eyes were reflective, like a cat's. That would explain his bold and confident strides through the growing murk. At least this time they didn't have to crawl. Night concealed them well enough, and sporadic gunplay covered Andrea's plodding steps and harsh breathing.

Blood followed their earlier trail precisely, his keen sight picking out every crushed blade of grass and knee-gouged mudhole. Parker would, he hoped, expect them to use a different route, and waste time looking for it.

At the edge of the clearing they plunged into a maze of thick, barely passable underbrush. The frantic run slowed to a deliberate, rhythmic trot, single file, Blood in the lead. The agent was fairly certain they hadn't been followed up to this point. If they were later stalked, he'd hear the hunters long before they were spotted. Blood wanted no more surprises.

Mud and humus lapped over their boot tops, and seeped through Andrea's cracked footwear. The reporter's panting was the loudest sound they made as they pushed on. After what seemed like several hours to the woman, Blood abruptly halted.

"W…." Andrea began.

A chilly finger brushed her lips, silencing her.

Blood pushed back the hair that normally concealed his slightly pointed ears, and strained his hearing to the fullest. Night birds chittered; frogs croaked; insects creaked. The gunfire, muffled by the trees, faded to a few weak, echoing pops, like the last gasp of a fireworks display. There was a suspicious but faint splash, probably made by an alligator slipping from its den, certainly too far away to pose an immediate threat.

"We can spare a few minutes," the vampire said, "if you want to catch your breath."

Andrea squatted in the mire without hesitation, heedless of the wet that seeped through her denim rags. "It isn't a question of wanting to," she gasped. "I can't take another five steps. My nerves are shot, I haven't slept in a week, I'm half starved, and this damned mud won't let go of my boots. I drag up half the state of Florida every time I raise a foot."

Blood merely grunted.

"We're following the shoreline of the hummock, aren't we?" Andrea asked. "I thought I saw water rippling by, back where the trees were thinner."

"Yes," Blood replied. "You should be safe here for the next few minutes."

She tensed. "Where are *you* going?"

"Scout ahead. Make sure I'm going the right way. We don't want to run in a circle back to the clearing."

Andrea shivered. "Don't go beyond my yelling range? Please?"

Blood removed his safari jacket and draped it over Andrea's exposed shoulders. She pulled it closed gratefully, oblivious of the hole in one shoulder, with the stiff dark patch below it.

"My hearing is excellent," the vampire replied.

Blood liked the idea of separating as little as she did, but Andrea *did* need to rest, and he felt he had to put the time to good use. A quick aerial survey would help him decide on the best way off the island, or at least the best way to avoid the fighting.

He walked just far enough to be out of Andrea's sight, and held his arms straight out. His snout began to grow, and the wings started to stretch from wrist to ankle, as his entire body became more compact. His clawed feet left the ground. He flapped straight up, to get free of the trees.

"Al," Andrea called, "I need you." The cry was not a scream but it ended shrilly, with an obvious note of terror. Blood cursed, folded his wings, and dropped rapidly. He was racing to her side even before the membranous tissue of his forelimbs was completely reabsorbed.

Andrea sat as he'd left her, but her shoulders were hunched tensely. He purposely stepped on a twig to let her know he was coming. She did not turn to face him. Her eyes were fixed on a low, black form slinking through the underbrush nearby.

Two orbs of brilliant yellow returned her gaze. At Blood's intrusion, they shifted toward him. The short muzzle bared deadly teeth.

The Florida panther was not known to attack humans without provocation, but Andrea looked like easy prey. With all the gunfire scaring the usual quarry, the beast was having an off night.

The vampire met, locked, and held those untamed eyes with his own feral glower. The cat found himself engaged in a battle of wills between feline and unhuman.

The panther's warning growl mingled with a chirrup of surprise. Blood growled back.

The animal blinked. He raised a forepaw, unsheathing five nasty-looking claws. Andrea whimpered, low in the back of her throat.

The panther licked the paw, turned, and padded silently away. The night was young.

"How did you scare him off?" Andrea asked.

Blood shook his head. "Did you see me do anything? Cats are unpredictable and independent. All the same, we'd better move."

Andrea rose slowly to her feet, her hands gripping the rough bark of a cypress for support. "You won't leave me again, will you? Out here, I mean?"

"No. We'll continue along the bank. Are you ready to walk again?"

She tested a shaky knee.

Before Andrea could reply, Blood lifted her as he had that morning. Privately, he was glad for her exhaustion. He could move faster and quieter carrying her weight than dragging it behind.

They'd gone about twenty paces when they heard the splash.

Andrea tightened her grip around Blood's shoulders, but no awful, mushy voice came out of the darkness. Still, Blood murmured, "Not an alligator."

"What do you mean, Al?"

Blood studied the woman's face. It was pale, muscles taut, and the eyes were wide, but not wild. Andrea Blanchard would see through a false note of optimism. Better to tell her how things stood than let her imagine the worst.

"I heard that noise before. I think it's someone poling a skiff, and getting closer. The Free Thought Alliance might be covering the escape routes."

Andrea licked her trembling lips. "Parker waded that stream to bring me here. Could it be him?"

"I doubt it," Blood replied. But it could. The vampire quickened his pace until he was racing through the arboreal shelter, though not at top speed. There were too many obstacles, and Andrea's body reduced his field of vision. Suprahuman reflexes alone saved them from more than one nasty spill over a malicious root or an unexpected fallen tree trunk.

An alligator crawled from the water and paused in their path. His long sleek head turned in the pair's direction. The jaws stretched open.

Blood leapt over the scaly back and kept going.

Suddenly the vampire had no purchase for his feet, as he plunged hip-deep into quicksand. The reporter, lulled almost to somnolence by the rhythmic pace, returned to full awareness at the feel of cold mud on her legs.

"Hey!" she exclaimed. "Did you decide we should swim for it or ... oh, Christ!"

Andrea tried to free her feet from the clinging ooze. She succeeded only in increasing the rate of sinking. Gently he lowered her limbs.

"Don't thrash about," she warned Blood. "If we stay calm, and move slowly, we can swim out of this."

Blood disagreed. Their combined weight, and the inertia of his plunge, pulled them down too fast. He's been taking long strides, almost flying. The lip could be five or six meters back, and who knew how far ahead? If solid ground could have easily been discerned from this muck, he wouldn't be in it.

At least he could get Andrea safely away.

He shifted the woman's weight, gripping her legs in one hand and upper back in the other. The movement plunged him shoulder-deep, but it tore her free. Andrea was held aloft over Blood's head, momentarily clear of the hungry mud.

"Hey!" she protested. "Didn't you hear what I ...?"

Suddenly she was flying backwards through the air. The rising moon seemed to spin. Her shoulder absorbed most of the impact as soft, densely packed vegetation cushioned her fall. She'd had just enough time, while hurtling, to cover her head with her arms for protection.

The shock passed quickly. She scrambled to hands and knees, stifling a spasm of coughing. Her hands shot out, desperately feeling for a root or limb long enough and strong enough to fish her rescuer from his doom.

Moonlight filtered between the leafy tree cover to illuminate the quicksand patch. Andrea stared numbly at its surface. Her hands clenched into fists.

Except for a rippling circle far beyond her reach, no sign remained of the man she knew as Al Cuardi. A cricket chirped gaily to her left, as though nothing had happened. Above the ripples fluttered a large bat, which then flew past her ear to vanish in shadows.

The splashing returned. Clearer. Closer. They'd lost what little lead they'd started with, or at any rate Andrea had paid that price. Al apparently had lost much more.

Andrea bit her lower lip, drawing a drop of blood. She would not be taken prisoner again. Not by Parker, not by the Alliance, not by a troop of Campfire Girls. She would rather drown beside the man who'd tried to save her.

The sound changed now. Mud squished beneath a weight

that moved slowly inland. The pursuer was no longer on the waterway.

Andrea rose on shaking legs. Her toes inched forward, feeling for the quicksand's edge. Her eyelids clamped shut, and her jaw trembled. Suicide was not an easy thing. Compared with what awaited her, however ....

She let her body fall stiffly forward.

A powerful arm clamped about her waist, dragging her back.

"Too long," she moaned. "I waited too long."

"I don't want to spend the rest of the night pulling you out of the same hole, Andrea," said Blood.

Her head swung around, eyes going wide. "Al?"

"More Jolson than Cuardi, at the moment." With his free hand, Blood wiped dripping mud from his face.

"How did you get out? I mean ..."

The footsteps grew louder. One set. The lone stalker was either very foolish, or very well armed.

"Quiet," Blood whispered.

He knew the footsteps were not heavy enough to be Parker's, and a moment later he received confirmation. The pursuer that burst from the foliage was half Parker's size and—despite an ugly machete in one hand, a pistol in the other, and field glasses apparently designed for three eyes on a neck strap—not exactly threatening.

"It's about time you idiots stopped," spat the newcomer. "I've been trying to catch up with you for twenty minutes."

Blood almost laughed. "Where the hell have you been, Hernandez?"

"Calling for the cavalry, you bean-pole." She holstered the gun and stepped forward, studying Blood's companion. "If you feel half as bad as you look, Andrea, it's no wonder you need help standing. How are you?"

Andrea could hardly speak. "Numb. We thought you were ... I mean...."

"We found the airboat," Blood explained.

Hernandez grinned sourly. "Yeah, that's really going to screw up my budget. But discretion is the better part of something or other. A handgun is no match for two guys in khaki, toting sniper rifles. There wasn't enough time to warm the motor so I lit out on foot before they saw me. Then the shooting started, and I decided reinforcements were definitely in order." As she led the two down to the bank, where her skiff was tied, the ranger added, "You'll think I'm silly, but I lost about an hour when that damned skunk-ape came traipsing along. I just couldn't deal with that, too."

"A wise precaution," Blood agreed, bending back a branch. "We've met him. Not a nice fellow."

"Him?" Hernandez asked.

Andrea merely nodded.

"This lady needs a safe place to rest," Blood said, changing the subject in a tone that said it should *stay* changed, for now. "She's been through a lot."

"No problem. She can bunk down in the ranger station."

"No!" His eyes flashed in the darkness.

Hernandez stopped and turned, one foot poised atop a mangrove root. "And why the hell not? It's comfortable. I've spent more than one night there myself."

"Too isolated. I want her away from the swamp completely. Get a motel room, and stay with her, or have someone you can trust stay with her."

The ranger frowned. "You going to tell me what's going on?"

"There isn't time. Ask Andrea later."

Hernandez looked from Blood to the reporter, and back again. "All right, Cuardi, I'll go along without an explanation. Only because I think you've got Andrea's welfare in mind above everything else. Don't worry. I'll see she gets to sleep if I have to tie her to the bed."

Andrea hissed, and her hands shot up like claws. "I'll kill the next person who comes near me with a rope."

Hernandez looked questioningly at Blood, startled by the reporter's vehemence. But the vampire was already on a new tack.

"You mentioned the cavalry. I take it you're referring to whoever's been shooting up the hummock tonight."

"I see," Hernandez said. "You can pump me, but I can't pump you."

"Come on, Hernandez."

The ranger sighed. "Yes, Cuardi, and if they haven't killed it yet they'll be setting the dogs on that stinking skunk-ape or whoever is running around in that Halloween costume."

"Your people sound a bit trigger-happy," Blood complained. "That could be dangerous in the dark."

"That thing," Hernandez snapped as she started for the stream again, "leapt from the brush, turned over a swamp buggy and crushed two Turnpike Troopers. That seemed sufficiently hostile to justify shooting at it." She used the machete on a vine that dangled across the trail. "Haven't seen a sign of those terrorist scum, though. I hope we haven't scared them off."

"Dead men don't scare easily."

The smell of the river grew strong in Blood's sensitive nostrils. Hernandez glanced back at the tall, pale-skinned agent with widening eyes. "You did that?"

"I wish I had. Your creature got there first, or at least he claims he did. Something else you can ask Andrea. Later."

The bow of the skiff had been dragged onto the muddy bank, so Blood had no difficulty helping Andrea on board. Hernandez guided the bedraggled reporter to the stem, where she replaced Blood's torn, filthy jacket with a clean blanket of thick brown wool. Andrea went along passively, too numb and exhausted even to speak a word of thanks. She was really getting out of this. She could still hardly credit it.

Blood took the jacket from Hernandez, and automatically brushed his fingers against the hidden inner pocket. The flat leather case containing alternate identification was still in place, next to his supply of bacteria-filled capsules. There was no real need to check, of course, since the pocket was too secure for anything to fall out, and he knew Parker hadn't found it because he'd used one of the capsules earlier.

"Hey, Cuardi! Want to give me a hand?" Hernandez was struggling with the bow of the skiff, trying to ease it into the stream. Her boots slid over the mud.

Blood stepped forward and gripped the ranger's arm. "Did anyone go inside the slave quarters?" he demanded.

"I have to row with that arm!" Hernandez snarled.

Blood realized he could feel the woman's humerus clearly through the well muscled arm. The slightest additional pressure of his fingers could snap the bone. He nodded, loosed his grip, and stepped back a pace. "It's vital, Hernandez. Did they?"

The ranger rubbed her biceps, wincing. "I don't know. When the shooting started, I borrowed this skiff and poled to our morning rendezvous, figuring you'd be there if you were still ... well, if you were anywhere. These infrared field glasses are great; I saw you coming clear as day, but then you...."

"Get Andrea out of here, fast!" Blood interrupted. He gave the skiff a prod with his toe that sent it drifting, and Hernandez waded frantically after it, with no opportunity to retort.

The vampire plunged into the underbrush, ignoring the machete-cut path and animal trails, in a direct line toward Parker's sanctum. If Deputy Grimm or any of his colleagues touched what was left on the table in Parker's laboratory, that person would be infected at once. It was not a good death; Blood had killed a man in the West Indies by that method, several years earlier. Worst than one person's agony, however, was the possibility that he or she would stumble outside before succumbing, and loose the bacteria on the swamp itself.

Nothing could stop its spread then. Nothing.

TWENTY-NINE

"I've faced death many times." protested Rodicio Chavez.

"Do as I say," Parker growled, "or you meet it for the last time here!"

Chavez licked his lips. They were in Parker's private quarters, standing awkwardly on two battered mattresses laid side by side. These provided the only clear space in a room lined with pyramids of books and equipment, boxes stuffed with yellowed news clippings, extracts of scientific papers, and scores of folders with reams of handwritten notes. To this had been added the weapons and supplies Chavez had helped salvage from the bodies of his former comrades before Parker buried them.

"You can do nothing against those policemen except get killed," Parker continued, as he filled a burlap bag with the day's lesser spoils: handguns, extra ammunition, grenades.

"Cops," Chavez sneered.

"I can deal with them myself," Parker went on, "but we can't stay here. I'll need your assistance to set up elsewhere. You're no use to me with a bullet in your brain."

Chavez raised his stumps. Closing his eyes, he could feel his fists clench in frustration. When he looked, there was only scarred and rounded flesh.

"Turn around," Parker ordered. "I'll have to tie this so it hangs in front. Otherwise the rope will choke you."

While the biologist fumbled with the knot, Chavez asked, "What if I see the girl or Cuardi?"

"Avoid them," Parker said firmly. "Especially Cuardi. There's something about him that isn't normal. Ah, that should hold!"

Chavez turned to face the monstrous Parker. He bent forward slightly, but the weight was not insupportable. The top of the burlap bag gaped slightly. Using his wrists like chopsticks, the terrorist fished out an automatic's clip, then let it fall back in.

"Your papers," the ex-Alliance man said. "Aren't you taking any of them?"

Parker laughed bitterly. He grabbed a thick folder from a box, scattering its contents except for a single sheet, which he held out for his assistant's examination. Even in the dim moonlight, Chavez saw the page was covered with meaningless scribblings. There was also a powerful moldy odor.

"This form has disadvantages," Parker explained. "I make notes out of habit, but can no longer read my own handwriting. No matter. The essentials are here." He tossed the sheet to the floor and pointed to his massive skull.

A searchlight beam penetrated the high, barred window, and vanished as quickly.

"You'd better get started," Parker warned. "They're regrouping from my last attack, but you should still be able to elude them. You know where to meet. I'll follow with the rifles as soon as I'm sure you're safe ... and I've prepared a surprise for our guests."

Chavez smiled at that. He shouldered open the door and vanished down the murky corridor.

Parker stacked the rifles in a pile in the center of the room, where he could scoop them up quickly. The guns were of no use to him as weapons, but he'd need money for new equipment. And Chavez knew where to sell them, or so he claimed.

In a storeroom next to his cell, Parker picked up a gallon container of kerosene. With his continually growing strength, he found it difficult to judge weight, so he unscrewed the cap to check that it was full. It was. He fumbled trying to put the cap back on, then tossed it aside. He was planning to use the whole container, anyway. His surprise called for running the generators at full power, and he didn't want any to run dry.

The lights in the laboratory glowed dimly, but they seemed bright as day compared to the darkness in the rest of the barracks. Parker halted a few steps inside the double room and stared at the operating table. He lowered the kerosene to the floor, where rubber sheeting accepted it silently. Another step nearer the table, and his liquid, pupil-less eyes widened with horror.

He was standing there still a moment later, when Blood said, "Hope you don't mind my dropping in uninvited."

Parker turned toward the vampire. Hatred gleamed in his bovine eyes. He raised a squamous arm, but not to strike a blow, not yet. A trembling gray finger pointed to the mass of swiftly dissolving flesh and bone, once the mutilated body of Frank Jordan, now a macabre centerpiece.

"You did this!" Parker accused. "You spoiled my greatest experiment!"

Blood wrinkled his nose. "Spoiled is right. You've got to expect that in these warmer climates. Now, with adequate refrigeration...."

"What is it, some type of organic acid? Not that it matters. I'd've had to terminate him, anyway, before I abandoned this place." Parker glared at the pale, gaunt man. "No doubt you're responsible for that, as well."

Blood stepped forward. "You're warped, Parker."

"Am I? You're in no position to criticize. I saw what you did to that youngster last night. Do you suppose Miss Blanchard would have accompanied you so readily if she'd known of your ghoulish habits?"

Blood ran his tongue over his fangs. "She wouldn't believe you."

"Why not? I know she dislikes me, but I've never lied to her. Where is she, by the way?"

"Where you can't get to her."

"Oh, dear. That sounds suspiciously like you gave her the same treatment."

He pointed at Jordan again. "You hoped I'd be careless enough to burn myself on that acid, didn't you?"

Blood smiled, as usual, unpleasantly. "I hadn't considered that. It's not a bad idea."

Parker grinned back. "It has its points."

It was easy to underestimate the reach of Parker's arms, and the speed with which he could move. There was a gray blur. The vampire felt his feet leave the rubber sheet carpeting. Before he could grapple with his assailant, Blood was propelled towards the operating table.

The agent twisted his body, falling short of the table. His temple grazed the sharp edge of a metal casing, and a thin trickle of crimson streaked his cheek. The bleeding stopped quickly, for though he'd fed recently, he hadn't fed well.

Parker was on Blood before he could regain his feet. Blunt fingers dragged him upright by the jacket collar. Fabric tore. Parker steadied his own bulk against a tall, solid piece of machinery and again pushed Blood at the nauseating remains of his fellow agent.

The vampire's hands shot out to clutch the lip of the metal table, saving him from immediate contamination. Parker was at his back, however, pressing forward and down, forcing Blood's face ever closer to the deadly mass.

The vampire turned his head, gaining a few centimeters of leeway. Parker bore down with his full weight, focusing his entire strength into the effort. Blood realized that Parker's brawn was equal, perhaps superior, to his own. Hand to hand combat was not the best strategy.

Suddenly, Blood was gone. Parker's own momentum carried him staggering forward, through a mysterious, intangible fog. He turned aside, but his right hand slid into the semi-liquid mess.

Recovering, Parker pulled free at once. There was a mild tingling in his palm, nothing painful. He studied it with horror and disgust, but also with scientific detachment. The scales on his palm seemed to be melting.

"Not acid," Parker muttered, puzzled.

Then the bacteria reached a nerve.

"It's alive!" Parker howled. He waved his hand violently, as if to dislodge something that clung to it. "It's alive and it's feeding!"

Blood solidified near the rubber-sheeted window, far from the snare of the spark collector. "Interesting, isn't it?" he asked.

The rough edges of Parker's mouth trembled. "It's eating me

faster than my cells can regenerate!"

Blood heard indistinct shouting from without. Some of Grimm's people had been close enough to hear Parker, and were coming to investigate.

Blood moved quickly to a doorway. He had to keep them out of this room.

Parker screeched, twisting in pain as the bacteria exposed more raw nerves to the fetid air, and spread up his wrist. His liquid eyes shifted frantically. He was doomed ... he was a dead man!

No, he realized, there was one chance. The microlife spread quickly, but they were still working on his lower right arm. If he could sever the limb, he would survive. A new arm would grow back in a week or two.

Parker smashed a glass cabinet with his left fist, fumbling with the selection of surgical knives within. One after another he threw them to the floor. Too short. Too small. Too thin. By the time he got halfway through the shoulder joint, his whole body would be infected.

Wait! In the storeroom ... a machete! One stroke of its long blade would solve his problem. He turned to the near door.

Blood barred his way.

Parker growled and lumbered forward, right arm extended. If Blood did not yield, if this delay cost Parker his life, as least he could take his killer with him.

But the pain slowed Parker's reflexes. Blood dodged him easily, and deflected him from the exit with a knee to the groin.

Behind that blow was the strength of twenty men.

Parker spun halfway around, kicking over the open kerosene tin. The volatile contents gurgled out, forming pools in the wrinkled rubber.

The vampire clasped his hands and smashed Parker at the base of his spine. An ordinary man would have been killed instantly. The creature staggered, crashing into a rough-hewn wooden table laden with electrical equipment. The impact transformed these to a heap of sputtering, smoking junk, and filled the room with blinding sparks. The spark collector could only absorb a minuscule portion of them. The brilliance even blinded the vampire, though his uncanny eyes quickly adapted in time to see, as though in slow motion, a huge blue spark arc directly toward the largest of the kerosene pools covering the floor.

THIRTY

Three men had been running toward the slave quarters when the first explosion knocked them off their feet. Sergeant Hector La Porta, who'd been closest, was grazed by a chunk of stone. A few centimeters lower, and his widow would have collected his pension. As it was, he lay stunned for several minutes.

When he came to, there was still plenty to look at. The second explosion seemed to engulf the building in a ball of fire, turning night to day on the isolated hummock. La Porta felt the heat sear his face. His two companions were already crawling away through the tall, vicious sawgrass, and he quickly followed.

Dodging falling fragments, Charlie Grimm raced to the fallen sergeant's side. La Porta's own handkerchief was saturated, dripping crimson. Grimm tossed it aside and used his own to bind the gash in La Porta's forehead.

"That's going to need several stitches, Hector," the deputy said, helping the man put more distance between them and the spreading circle of fire. Bill Arneson was already shouting orders to cut down sawgrass as a firebreak, and several Guardsmen slung rifles over their shoulders and drew machetes to obey. "Damn," La Porta said. "Those needles sting!"

"All right, this is far enough. Lay still. You may have a concussion." One of La Porta's companions, a skinny young man with a thick black mustache, hurried over. "Christ, Hector," he cried, "I didn't even see you! I wouldn't have left you back there!"

"What the hell were you clowns doing, anyway?" Grimm barked suddenly. "I gave strict orders for no one to go near that building until I got back."

"We heard the skunk-ape, Charlie," La Porta replied. "He must've been inside the whole time."

Grimm scowled, scrubbing the blood from his hands with a fistful of dirt. "No wonder we couldn't find the thing."

"I saw something," said the other man. "Just before it blew. I think."

"You *think*?" Grimm repeated.

"Looked like a big dog right outside the entrance."

Grimm frowned. "Some of the trackers slipped their leashes. I guess that one found the scent first. Poor beast."

"He might've gotten away," came a voice behind Grimm. "If he ran fast enough."

Grimm turned and rose to confront a tall, thin man with pale skin and sleek black hair. Dried mud streaked the new-comer's face and safari jacket, which also boasted bloodstains and a bullet hole at one shoulder. His expression could mean anything, but his bearing was impressive despite his appearance. "Who the hell are you?" the deputy growled.

Blood had already removed the leather case from its secret, inner pocket. He handed it to Grimm, who glanced at it cursorily. "Victor Varney," he read, "Special Services. Another Fed. As if the one we already have wasn't enough trouble."

Blood smiled slightly. "That would be Allen Davies."

"You know him?"

"I know of him. You have my sympathies."

Grimm lifted an eyebrow. "Sounds like you know him, all right. Captain Miranda should really be running this show, but he's back at the swamp buggies trying to keep Davies too busy to bother us. I'm in charge until someone more qualified shows. I suppose you think you're it?"

Blood shook his head. "Not me. You seem to be doing fine."

"Yeah?" Unable to detect any sarcasm in the agent's voice, Grimm softened. "Well, maybe, considering we got off to a bad start." He looked glumly at the burning building. "Damned if I know what to do next, though."

"Can I do anything to help?"

Grimm rubbed a jowl in thought, leaving a trail of dirt and blood. "Nothing I can think of now. I'd've liked a good look at those ruins, but by the time we get fire-fighting equipment out here there won't be enough left to fill a matchbox. Might as well let it burn out."

Blood scanned the thick surrounding vegetation, which glowed orange with reflected light. "Is that safe?"

Grimm smiled indulgently. "I can tell you're no cracker. This won't spread far, not in this damp ground. We wouldn't even bother cutting back, except to give our people a chance to get away. The Forestry people usually let this kind of fire run its course, part of the natural process. Sometimes they even start fires themselves. Confuses the hell out of tourists."

Blood nodded, watching the flames rise higher. Thick clouds of smoke began to obscure the moon. Three more machete-wielders joined Ameson's group. "How's Sheriff Rudge doing?" Blood asked.

"Still critical, but improving." Grimm turned quizzically to the questioner. "I thought I recognized your voice. What's your name, Varney or Cuardi?"

"Depends. Right now you don't need a reporter."

"I guess not. I'll be damned. You must have been tracking the Free Thought Alliance yourself."

Blood shaded his eyes, saying nothing.

"Well," Grimm continued, "I don't think that group's going to bother anyone any more. We found about twenty fresh graves over by those trees."

"You're sure they're in those graves?"

"We only took the time to dig up one, but he certainly dressed the part. I hope we can persuade Collins to give us some positive identifications. I'd like to be sure of *something* out of this whole mess!"

"Here's something you can be sure of," came a new voice.

The flames played across Rodicio Chavez's tormented, half-ruined face, giving him a demonic look. His arms were stretched forward, level with his breastbone. Braced between the scarred stumps was a US Army hand grenade, its serrated body glittering with menace. A duck of his head, and his teeth could clamp down on the pull ring and yank out the pin. Combined with the bagful of grenades and ammunition, it would make quite a blast.

Chavez glared at the vampire. "He warned me about you, Cuardi. Now you've killed him, you and these pigs. If I could, I would destroy every man on this island. But I will settle for those in my range, especially you."

Hector La Porta staggered erect, aided by his friend. "Who the devil are you?"

"Don't you ever read wanted flyers, Hector?" said Grimm. "That's Rodicio Chavez."

"Ready to give yourself up, Chavez?" asked Blood.

"Funny man."

"Be reasonable, Chavez," said Grimm. "Your Alliance is broken. You've no place to turn. In prison you'll get decent health care, prostheses and the training to use them."

The terrorist's eyes seemed to glitter. "My one chance to be a whole man has been destroyed. I could have had hands again, real ones, not dead things of plastic and metal. We could have saved humanity in spite of itself!"

"He's insane," La Porta said.

"Keep him talking," Blood whispered. "Buy us time." The vampire glimpsed the shadowy figure before the other three, but soon all four were staring intently at the terrorist's face, fearful of betraying Captain Miranda with a single stray glance. In another minute, perhaps two, the trooper would be close enough for a headlock that would prevent Chavez from pulling the pin.

"I don't understand," Grimm said. "How could you possibly have flesh and bone hands again?"

"Cuardi knows. Ask him. But you'll have to be fast."

"I asked you. What is it, some new grafting technique?"

Chavez chuckled. "Nothing so crude, pig."

Blood interrupted. His voice was low and even. "All right, Rodicio. Relax. We'll work something out. You want to relax, don't you? Rest those weary arms? Wouldn't you like to sleep?"

"We'll all be sleeping soon enough," Chavez spat. But his single eye blinked several times. The hypnosis was taking hold.

Captain Miranda poised to leap the final meter.

"Drop it, Chavez!" shouted a man in a gray, pinstriped suit, running up behind Miranda. "You're surrounded!"

Grimm groaned.

Miranda yelled, "Davies, you shithead!"

Rodicio pulled the pin with his teeth.

Everyone flattened, heads down. Even Davies.

Except for Blood.

The vampire's boots pounded the marshy ground. How much delay was there on the grenade's fuse? Five seconds? Seven? To grab the pineapple and toss it safely away would take split second timing with no preparation. No second chances if he missed the first time.

But there was a bigger target.

Chavez suddenly found himself flying through the air, two meters above the waving sawgrass, and the burlap bag had been torn from his neck. He let the grenade fall, but by then he was past killing range of the men he'd felt had stolen his last chance for a normal life.

The grenade exploded half a meter above the ground, spraying metal shards and muck, but claiming only a single victim.

Rodicio Chavez.

Blood knelt beside Deputy Grimm, and helped the heavy-set man to his feet. Grimm's face was as white as the vampire's.

"We're not dead?" he asked in a terrified whisper.

"You're not," Blood replied. "The charge must have been defective. That's the chance you take, buying illegal weapons. Unfortunately for Chavez, it wasn't a complete dud."

Captain Miranda sat up slowly. He was sure the grenade had gone off some distance from where Chavez had originally stood, where only a lumpy burlap bag now remained, but he was too relieved to care. Since he was closest, except for Davies, whose head was still down but whose rump was in the air, he decided to take a look at the body.

Chavez lay on his back, his single eye shut and teary. A thick mat of sawgrass had cushioned his fall. He looked just as satanic dead as alive.

The terrorist's chest moved.

"God damn!" Miranda exclaimed. "The son of a bitch is still alive!"

Blood reached the Captain's side first, followed by Grimm and Davies.

Rodicio Chavez had survived another explosion, but not without cost. His arms were studded with shrapnel, and his right leg and left foot were gone.

"Jesus!" Grimm said. "You're the toughest bastard I've *ever* seen."

"Guess he won't be climbing out of any windows this time," Davies said.

"We'll play it safe," Miranda snarled. "This time you won't be there."

"Just what the hell does that mean?" Davies snapped.

Miranda ignored him, turning to the deputy with a wide smile. "I was coming to tell you what Commissioner Weinberg told my office, Charlie. Just got the call a few minutes ago. You see, the FBI and the Cleveland police force arranged for Rodicio Chavez to escape so he would lead them to the rest of the Alliance. Instead, Davies let Chavez slip through their net almost immediately."

"That's a lie!" Davies shouted. "Don't say another word! It could have happened to anyone. Sheriff, arrest this man for treason!"

"As a result," Miranda continued coolly, "Davies was dismissed from the Bureau."

Grimm took a firm grip on Davies's lapels and spun the young man around. "Impersonating a federal agent ought to be good for a few years, Davies. What was that about treason?"

"I'm with the Treasury Department. Alcohol, Tobacco, and Firearms. It's practically the same thing!"

"We'll let Washington decide that, shall we?" Grimm turned to the gathering crowd. "Hey, someone stop this man's bleeding, will you? I've got a bodacious lot of questions to ask."

"You won't get any sensible answers," Blood warned.

"I'll settle for any kind of answer, at this point."

Blood shrugged. "One more thing, Deputy."

"Can I deny a man who's just saved my life? Ask."

The vampire tongued his lowered canines. "I'd like to take Davies in."

"I'm afraid," interrupted Captain Miranda, "that isn't Charlie's decision, Mr. Cuardi."

"Varney. Cuardi's a cover name." He reached for his leather case. "I have authority."

"So have I, from Commissioner Weinberg. I also have sore feet and a splitting headache, and this is one pinch I'd like in my record. If you want to argue jurisdiction, come to my office in the morning. Maybe we can work something out."

Blood seethed inwardly. He wanted more than custody, and he wanted it now! Blood had promised himself he'd deal with Davies if the opportunity arose. Even now, he could snatch the young man from Grimm's grip, outrun everyone on the hummock, and deal with Davies as he saw fit.

He resisted the impulse. Davies was well on his way to destroying himself, and the vampire could be content with that for now. His guardian angel on the Security Committee would have a hard time explaining this bit of duplicity. "That's all right, Captain, he's all yours."

Miranda accepted the concession with a dignified nod, and clamped his handcuffs on the Treasury man.

"You'll regret this!" Davies warned.

"I know I will," Miranda said, leading him away. "I should just shoot you."

Grimm breathed a sigh of relief. He looked at Blood and grinned wryly. "Now I *know* I'll never find out what went down here tonight."

Blood stared at the brilliant orange and yellow flames rising from the site of the Holroyd ruins. Walls that had stood more than a century collapsed in minutes. Black smoke curled up from sawgrass patches ignited by flying cinders. "Perhaps not, Deputy. But it certainly looks like it's over."

"I hope so," Grimm admitted. "I've seen enough deaths in one day to last me a lifetime."

The unpleasant smile crossed Blood's face again, but glare and shadow hid it from Grimm. He recalled how little blood had been in Jordan's corpse, and how his teeth had ached at the thought of taking Davies somewhere alone. Perhaps, he thought, just one more death for tonight. There must be a poacher or escaped convict or just plain fool wandering the marshlands somewhere. He'd earned a bit of sport.

ABOUT THE AUTHOR

Gordon Linzner is founder and former editor/publisher of *Space and Time Magazine*. He is the author of the novels *The Spy Who Drank Blood, The Oni,* and *The Troupe*, as well as dozens of short stories appearing in *Fantasy & Science Fiction, Twilight Zone, Sherlock Holmes Mystery Magazine*, and numerous other magazines and anthologies

Curious about other Crossroad Press books?
Stop by our site:
http://store.crossroadpress.com
We offer quality writing
in digital, audio, and print formats.

www.ingramcontent.com/pod-product-compliance
Lightning Source LLC
Chambersburg PA
CBHW021248170626
46808CB00011BA/2337